THE MOUNTIE IN THE HOUSE
AND OTHER STORIES

RICK BUTLER

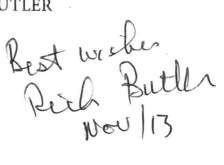

Best wishes,
Rick Butler
Nov/13

Agio
PUBLISHING HOUSE

151 Howe Street, Victoria BC Canada V8V 4K5

All characters appearing in this work are fictitious.
Any resemblance to real persons, living or dead,
is purely coincidental.

Cover art by Lorena Ziraldo
Images on pages 31, 47, 65, 77, 95, 107, 127,
143, 157, 191 and 203 from istockphoto.com
The other images are in the public domain or
from the author's collection.

Rick Butler may be contacted at
hotelcaliforniadude@yahoo.com

For rights information and bulk orders, please contact us at
www.agiopublishing.com

The Mountie In The House
ISBN 978-1-897435-92-2 (trade paperback)
ISBN 978-1-897435-93-9 (casebound)
Also available as a Kindle ebook

Cataloguing information available from
Library and Archives Canada.
Printed on acid-free paper.
Agio Publishing House is a socially responsible company,
measuring success on a triple-bottom-line basis.
10 9 8 7 6 5 4 3 2 1f

To TLP, *my constant muse*

AUTHOR'S FOREWORD
(with thanks to François Rabelais)

Readers, Friends, if you open these pages
put your prejudices aside.
There's nothing here that's outrageous,
sick, bad, or contagious.
Not that I'm puffed up with pride,
For in this book all you'll find is laughter
and the occasional surprise.

ALSO BY RICK BUTLER

Quebec: The People Speak
(Doubleday, 1978)

The Trudeau Decade
(Doubleday, 1979)

Vanishing Canada
(Irwin Publishing, 1980)

The story *An Almost Perfect Afternoon*
(Published in *The Antigonish Review* 2010)

The story *A Seaside Romance or Two*
(Published in *The Nashwaak Review* 2011)

CONTENTS

EVERY PICTURE TELLS A STORY...

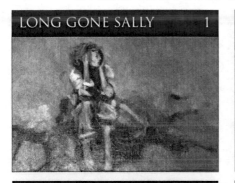

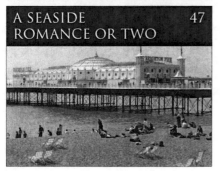

CONTENTS

EVERY PICTURE TELLS A STORY...

THE MOUNTIE IN THE HOUSE
AND OTHER STORIES

LONG GONE SALLY

Anatomy of a Bad Goodbye

I always felt it was our house, even if Carl and I never owned the joint. You rent a place you really love for three years—spend over a thousand nights there, dream a ream of dreams there, eat a couple thousand meals there, listen to a freakin' library of music there, make love a whole lotta times there, cry a tiny stream of tears there—it becomes your home. Know what I mean? And our street—why, you never saw such a cute, quiet little street. A pedestrians-only walkway from the 1920s right here in the heart of hippy dippy Venice, California. Peace out, people! Most of the time....

I made my jewelry in that two-storey yellow clapboard house with the white picket fence all around it like Indians circling a wagon train— while Carl just raised Hell. That's what he did best. And that's exactly how Carl and I met—Carl all jacked up on vodka and OJ rollerblading up to my jewelry stand on the Venice Boardwalk that sunny Saturday from Hell. Oh yeah, that's how it all started.

"Sweet thing! How much you want for the whole bunch of it?" he said, looking down at my display like he already owned it. Seventy-five pieces laid out there.

"More than you got, big talker," I said.

People used to say I was refreshingly honest. Other people said I had a big mouth. Guess they were both right. Carl just laughed through that gorgeous year-round tan and those gleaming white teeth. Goddamn Carl. Next thing you know, we're sweethearts-in-residence on the Venice walk streets.

That house of ours—Norman Rockwell normal on the outside, very Hieronymus Bosch on the inside. Know him? Freaked-out Dutch painter from the 1500s—painted parties and orgies that make those Playboy Mansion parties look like Rotary Club luncheons. We weren't into the orgy thing, but everything else was fair game—coke, grass, pills, booze—anything Carl could lay his tattooed hands on, and I could help him pop, snort or guzzle. A thousand days and nights in our crazy love nest in the Wild West. Tupac got it right—California knows how to party! California knows how to party! Yes, it does and yes, we did!

Hard and fast like an elevator with a snapped cable. Whoop! Whoop! Until our nonstop joyride came to an end that moonlit Tuesday ten years ago right around 2 a.m. Nothing much happens on Tuesdays, you say? Wrong! That final Tuesday, a very drunk, pilled-up Carl decided he'd had enough of my refreshing honesty.

"Shut your fucking mouth! Just shut the fuck up!"

Kept repeating it like some messed up mantra. Explaining things was never one of Carl's strengths. And listening to others when I was drunk or stoned wasn't one of mine. And remember out here on my own, I had no family or old friends to turn to for a little advice. And I could have used some. Bad combination, bad moment. I laughed in his face. *BAM!* Carl clocked me across the head with an empty champagne bottle—those things are thick and heavy. Bottle smashes, Sally goes down hard, Carl climbs the stairs to bed alone.

"And keep it shut!"

Oh, I kept it shut all right. Forever. *Thanks a bunch, Carl.*

Couple days later, Carl tells the neighbors I moved out in the dead of night without so much as a good-bye—'cause I was a gold digger. Said I met some businessman from the South Bay with a briefcase and a BMW. Yeah, right—if I was such a gold digger, why'd I ever take up with Mr. Underachiever? But what's it matter now? Carl and I are through, finally and forever. But that yellow house and white picket fence haunt me, they really do. Stand for something good that might have been. *Sometimes, America—yes, I'm talking to you—sometimes I think we'd all be so much better off if we were Mormons or Muslims and didn't drink or drug at all. How calm, how decent, how sensible would we be? Arguing about who should take out the trash or do the dishes—stuff like that. But, no, we gotta have it all, do it all, crash into each other in the fast lane—don't we, America? And where does all that partying get us? Cold and forgotten. I'm telling the simple truth here, if anybody'd care to listen.*

Carl stumbles downstairs next morning all hung over and disbelieving. Kneels down beside me, turns me over gently, touches my cold clammy forehead, starts blubbering like a baby. "Baby, Baby! No, Baby, no! Wake up!" Tells me how much he loves me. How he never meant for this to happen. How sorry he is. Right. Sorry enough to call my family, our friends, the police? Oh, no, Carl's too busy for that. Gotta get to the Home Depot and pick up some cleaning supplies, Ready Mix concrete, a shovel— *Thank you, Carl: duly noted. Helluva way to say good-bye.*

Ten years pass. Random tenants come and go: a hot young actor, a bloated film critic, a cat-loving divorcee, a home-based psychologist—single people. Then came the lawyers in love, just-married thirty-somethings from North Carolina. All white and bright and filled with deeeelight to be in the land of palm trees and litigation. Their very own piece of paradise. Ouch! That hurt. Because they were living the life Carl and I were supposed to be living. There's this Tim McGraw song about this guy whose wife kicks him out, then he has to watch her new boyfriend take over his house and old life, right down to the kids and family dog. Those lawyer lovebirds took over my house and my old life like that. Made me crazy jealous. Damn if they didn't invite the neighbors over for drinks and dinner soon as they unpacked. Started with this screenwriter guy named Teller and his wife just down the street. Lifted up the area rug in the living room and showed them the floor where the outline of somebody's torso was still visible on the blood-stained hardwood. Now I'm a freakin' tourist attraction? Time for me to move on, you say? Find closure? Get on with a wonderful after-life? Oh, really? How would you feel lying in concrete under the back lawn?—no funeral, no family or friends mourning you, no obituary, no tombstone—just a big old unsolved mystery. A "missing person."

Meanwhile, the lawyers in love are dining out on their new patio furniture four feet overhead, yapping their Southern heads off about what a great house and neighborhood they scored. You'd be pissed, too. Carl? Vanished—who knows where. The fact he laid me in the ground all teary-eyed and blubbering with a kiss on the cheek doesn't matter a damn. Where was all that tenderness while I was alive? Carl was crying for himself, not me. Scared shitless he'd get caught.

—m—

Lay down, Sally, and rest you in my arms, sang Eric Clapton. *Don't you think you want someone to talk to?*

That was our song. But not any more. *Carl—you listening to me? I'm tracking your sorry ass down.*

But how? First there's the matter of my missing body, undiscovered in a concrete dress these ten years. No body, no crime, and no crime, no justice. My parents are still holding onto the thinnest thread of hope, my friends have given up altogether, my old customers are buying from my competitors on the beach, the lawyer lovebirds are nesting in my home... and me? One restless spirit. No peace. But what can you do from this invisible limbo? Well, let me tell you....

Us restless spirits exude a force field we can use to mess with anything electronic: turn the radio and TV on and off, shut down the iPods, create static, that sort of thing. I'd turn the radio to the country station 97.3 FM whenever that Tim McGraw song was on, or interfere with their TV movies at a critical point, or mess with their alarm clock to make them late for work—good for a few laughs. But you gotta be cool about it—not overdo it—or they'll think there's a ghost in the house and if they're Catholic like me, they might even call in a priest for an exorcism. Huge headache.

Female lawyer in love sensed my presence. "George, there's something strange going on in this house...."

"Of course, dear—this is Venice Beach! Maybe the ghost of Jim Morrison raiding the liquor cabinet?"

"Don't be making ghost jokes," she said. "Every house has a history. This place is eighty years old. There's worldly history and the other-worldly kind."

"Maybe we should call in Ghostbusters?" he said.

"Stop that!" said Serious One.

I needed a plan to draw attention to myself there in the cold, cold ground. One fine Friday, it came to me in the form of a Home Depot TV commercial for this new outdoor in-ground Jacuzzi. If I could just get the lawyers to buy that thing, they'd have to dig a big old hole in the backyard and—

I started playing that commercial over and over for them—drove them to change from Dish TV to Time Warner. Didn't help. Until she said the magic words: "George, maybe we should just get that Jacuzzi. At least we'd be in the backyard soaking and stroking and away from that damn TV."

Good call, Southern Girl. Advertising works.

It was coming up on Christmas when they sprang for the Jacuzzi and called in Dante the hippie contractor to dig up the backyard. We knew Dante—Carl had called him years ago to replace that front window Carl had thrown a chair through. So the guy knew me! Of course, Dante was into weed and mescaline and the Grateful Dead on the iPod and working to music, so that Jacuzzi hole was getting dug in slow-mo time. Me? Like a debutante getting ready for her coming out party! The lawyers in love invited the four parents up from North Carolina to celebrate Christmas. *Welcome, y'all! Have we got a holiday surprise for you!*

—⁓—

Dante struck concrete and chipped through to my flannel shirt right about 1 p.m. on December 22nd.

Hey, Dante! Guess who?! ID me to the cops and we're done, OK?

That freak majorly freaked out. The lovebirds and their parents were having a nice lunch when Dante came bug-eyed to the back door.

"Wow, man—you gotta see something…"

Two hours later: yellow police tape all around the property, investigators combing over everything, news 'copters overhead, front page of the *L.A. Times* next morning. My fifteen minutes of fame. Just one problem: after ten years in the ground nobody knew it was me. Not a good feeling. The first detective on the scene questioned Dante. "Any idea who she might be? The remains have been here quite some time."

Dante was shaking like a marijuana leaf in a shitstorm. "Hey, man, I have trouble remembering last week, let alone last year..."

One useless hippie. *Don't remember me? The girl you toked up with after fixing that front window? The girl you put the move on while Carl was passed out upstairs and I never told Carl, never made it difficult for you? The girl whose jewelry business paid your bill? Thanks a lot, dude. Peace out...*

LAPD didn't have a lot to go on. No wallet, no fingerprints, no DNA record in the public database, no neighbors after all those years to ID me. A long way from Vanishing Carl. But this investigation still had one trump card: Homicide Detective Calafati, my knight in shining armor. God bless him. All young and trim and handsome and caring. He actually spoke to me when we found ourselves alone. "Don't you worry, my girl. We'll find out who you are and who put you here. In your Neil Young hippie plaid shirt. All five feet of you—doesn't look like a fair fight to me. Don't you worry—I'll get the bastard."

He cared. That's the best kind of cop you're ever going to find; they just don't come any better. Now here's the coolest thing—Calafati's father was one of those Mounties up in Canada. He told me the Mounties' motto is *The Mounties Always Get Their Man*, and that's what he lived by. My very own Mountie built a murder case around a cigarette pack— Camel menthols in the front pocket of my shirt. Not a common smoke.

Calafati takes that pack around to the five convenience stores within walking distance—asks if they remember a five-foot female customer ten years or so back with brown hair, maybe dressed like a hippie, who smoked those.

On the fifth try—bingo! Owner of Joe's Liquor on Lincoln: "Sure. Sally from the neighborhood. Smoked like a chimney, drank that cheap Merlot. Good customer. Then one day—gone."

"Remember who she lived with?"

"Nope. Always came in here alone. Good luck. She was a cheerful one," said Joe.

He remembered me. That means something. Those kings and queens and presidents—they've got their statues and paintings and pages in the history books. Me? I've got a dark stain on somebody's living room floor, and a detective who cares. Despite all his washing and scrubbing and huffing and puffing, Carl couldn't get my blood completely outta those floorboards.

"Goddamn you, Sally! Goddamn mess!" Carl actually complained while trying to wash me away. Can you believe it? Prick. You never know somebody's true colors until they win the lottery or face a murder rap. Now the screenwriter from down the block who had viewed my bloodstains got really interested. Thought the whole affair would make a great TV movie. Pitched a title around town: MURDER IN YOUR OWN BACKYARD. Sold it to HBO. *Thank you, Hollywood, Thank you, Teller—any royalties here for Long Gone Sally?* Oops. Royalties? Forgot I was dead there for a minute. *Could I at least get a "based on a true story" credit?* I never played the fame game, but hey, this is L.A, after all!

Next Calafati tracked down the old Jew who had the house ten years back, when it was a rental property. Did he remember Carl?

"Schmuck! How could I forget? Late rent every time. Bounced checks. Late-night parties. Slip and fall claims. Bankruptcy proceedings. Oy! His name? Yeah, I got his name right here. Schmuck. Carl Schmuck! Just kidding—Carl Colson. Somebody do him in? Say yes, Detective! Send me to my grave a happy landlord…"

Detective Calafati found Carl eighty miles away, cooling his shitheels these past five years on an aggravated assault charge at Lompoc maximum security. Perfect. Seems I wasn't the only one Carl coldcocked when they weren't looking. Calafati brings the news back to Venice where I'm still staying until I'm laid to rest in Kansas.

"You actually located her killer?" said Mr. Lawyer in Love, all white and bright beside his perfect wife.

"Sure did," said Calafati.

I'm floating over the kitchen table, happy as Casper the Friendly Ghost. This is a big day!

"In Lompoc doing time for another crime. He admitted everything," Calafati said.

"Open and shut case," says Captain Obvious across the table.

Only it wasn't quite so obvious.

"Not quite. Seems her boyfriend Carl got into an argument with the wrong inmate shortly after entering prison. Got himself thrown off a third-level balcony, landed on his head. Not competent to stand trial."

How sweet is that? Rough justice served on Carl in my absence!

Hey—I'm rockin' and reelin'! I turn on the radio *loud* to that Lionel Ritchie song *Dancing On the Ceiling.*

"Damn, there it goes again! I swear, this place is haunted!" says Mrs. Lawyer.

"Makes a nice change from Tim McGraw though," says Happy Hubby.

"May I ask what in the world you two are talking about?" said Calafati.

The detective called my parents back in Kansas. They talked for a good half-hour, and I was privileged to listen in. Mom and Dad were so grateful to finally know what had happened to me, even though they'd kept that thin thread of hope alive all these years. There's no well deeper than a parent's love, and I was basking in it fully. Mom and Dad are the best, that's all there is to it. Calafati told them he would make all necessary arrangements to send me back home. I played that Merle Haggard song on the kitchen radio soon as the lawyers split for dinner: *Sing me back home/ With a song I used to hear...*

—◊—

Thank you, Detective. For giving a damn.

It was a real nice service at our little church back in Kansas. All my family and old friends were there. Then we drove together to the family plot Grandpa and Grandma set aside all those years ago—me in this big shiny hearse. *Now this is going to sound strange, America: an invitation to your own funeral isn't exactly a sought-after thing. But if you're ten years dead like me, it's a hot ticket.* See, there's no peace without it. It's like this: every baby deserves a christening, every high school grad deserves a prom, every bride deserves a wedding in white and every stiff deserves a proper send-off. I'd been waiting ten years for my funeral, remember. No spirit is ever at rest without a proper farewell. Everyone's gotta be there: your family, spouse, old lovers, friends, high school buds, all the important people in your life. Admit it: it's cool to be the centre of attention! Just kidding—but without a proper send-off, you'll be left wandering the spirit world forever. Sleepless, haunted, like some refugee from the graveyard scene in that Michael Jackson *Thriller* video. You want that kind of eternity for yourself? Of course you don't. I mean there's quality of life—and quality of afterlife. Take it from someone who knows.

—⁂—

My special day got me to thinking about what we leave behind. You know—our legacy. We all leave footprints, large or small. If I'd been more mindful of that, I'd have made more of an effort along life's highway—been kinder, been more generous, lived up to certain expectations, listened to certain criticisms, moved through the days and nights of my life with a little more grace. Look, I'm not preaching here—just groping for a clearer view of this passing parade we call life.

One last thing, America: up here in the heavens, we get a peek at what you're doing down there in the "real" world. I'm not kidding. You're totally entertaining. The ultimate reality TV. So listen up. There's this attractive young lady from my hometown I've been following lately. She's a little louder, spunkier, flashier, more inclined to run with the party crowd. Remind you of anybody you might know? She does? Then please—keep an eye on that young lady, OK? Especially on those warm summer nights, when she's out there movin' and groovin', meetin' and greetin'—just being herself. Young One doesn't know the true power—in her glance, in her smile, in her walk. Not to mention everything else in her feminine arsenal. So keep a kind eye on that charmer. Spare her a little of your time, attention, well-chosen advice. Don't let her wander unthinkingly towards places and people she'd be better off avoiding.

What I'm trying to say is: just be a friend to her. That's all. **We could all use one more real friend, right?**

The End

… of Sally's silence.

THE MOUNTIE IN THE HOUSE
The RCMP and Me

When you're eleven and your dad's a Mountie—a Royal Canadian Mounted Policeman—it's kind of a big deal. When new kids learn who your dad is, they treat you different right away. The guys go all quiet and make sly little jokes like, "Gotta be on your best behavior every day, eh?"

The girls get the opposite way—all talkative and giggly like, "Oh, a Mountie! Does he wear his uniform around the house? Where does he keep his gun at night?"

Dumb questions. But that's OK, because they're all just jealous, and I'm proud of my dad. Everybody knows the RCMP motto: *The Mounties Always Get Their Man.*

They're not just cops—they're Mounties!

The neatest thing about having a Mountie for a dad is the police stories he tells you at home. I used to take some of the best ones to school and tell them to the other kids. They really liked them! After a while, they even gave me a nickname because of Dad's stories. They called me Teller, the guy who tells the stories, and it stuck. Now everybody calls me Teller.

When you're a Royal Canadian Mountie, they move you around a lot—what Dad calls "broadening your horizons." Then he winks. He got all the horizon-broadening he ever needed during the Second World War, he says, when they sent him overseas for five years. That's why Dad never really liked my mom's brother who never fought in the war.

"What I never understood about your uncle," said Dad, "is if he liked dressing up in a Shriners uniform so much, why didn't he put on a Canadian army uniform?"

He'd say it with a smile but he was serious. Dad said keeping our own troops in line on a Saturday night overseas was a lot tougher than fighting the Germans. I wouldn't know much about that, but I do know how happy my father was when the RCMP moved us to this little village of Sherbrooke, Nova Scotia: Population 375—including the three of us. Dad says it reminds him of the village he grew up in way over in Ireland. Mom told me he left Ireland when he was twenty because he didn't get along with his own father, who was this big landowner and senator and kinda mean to my father, which I don't like to hear because Dad's never been mean to me or anybody else. Dad's over six feet tall and broad in the shoulders and he got into this big argument with The Senator, who pushed him through a tall window in the dining room of their house over there. I guess my father didn't fight back because he didn't want to whup my grandfather in front of everybody. Mom said not to talk about my dad's father, which is fine with me 'cause Dad and I have plenty to talk about on our own—like the Little People.

The little people are the leprechauns living in the forests of the Old Country, playing tricks on each other and searching for this pot of gold.

"They don't like being called 'leprechauns,'" said Dad. "They prefer 'little people.' And they're quite wary of us, which is why they live deep in the forest."

"Why? People wouldn't hurt them, would they?" I said.

"They think we're after their gold, Teller," said Dad.

"Is there a pot under every rainbow?" I said.

"See?" said Dad. "That's exactly what the little people are worried about, young man—gold diggers with too many questions."

I totally believed it all until two years ago—but what the heck! Are you mad at your parents over Santa and the Elves? Dad just gave me a whole second set of sawed-off rascals to dream about. Dad's sort of our homegrown Walt Disney. Except when he gets mad, which he did the other day when Brian Davis and me were throwing snowballs at cars driving past our house. We nailed this big black Buick smack on the windshield—*whack!!* The driver stopped right there in the road, and we hightailed it back to the house. He comes to the front door while we're upstairs acting super normal and tells Dad his windshield has a crack. Dad calls us downstairs and sees the truth right there on our faces. He's in his pressed Mountie shirt and blue tie and gold tie clip. The driver's embarrassed to even be complaining about a Mountie's son. So he says, "Well, boys will be boys."

Oh, really? Then why stop and jump out of your fancy car and stand there giving me and Brian such a hard time? I'm thinking it, not saying it. Dad takes out his wallet and offers to pay for the windshield, which really embarrasses the guy! He starts doing this funny backward two-step off the porch and down the steps: "Boys will be boys! Boys will be boys!" All the way down. Like I said, people act funny around a Mountie.

Then Dad puts on his blue coat and big round Mountie hat. "Get in the car."

We trudge through the falling snow to the black '52 Chevy with the white doors and light on the roof. To me it was always sorta like the family Batmobile. Not today: all of a sudden it's Hell's Chariot taking us on a one-way trip down to the flames of eternal damnation. Dad opens the back door: a very bad sign, 'cause I always ride up front. He pulls out and heads through town. Sherbrooke's a mile long; we're at one end, Brian's yellow house is in the middle, and now we're driving.

"You passed my house, Mr. Clancy."

Like he didn't notice? Wake up, Brian...

"Where we going?" asks my fearful friend.

"Straight to jail. Destruction of private property."

Brian starts bawling like a baby right there in the backseat. "Oh, no, Mister Clancy, please! Don't take us to jail! Dad will kill me! I won't do it ever again! I promise! I promise! Please!"

I'm wondering if Brian ever heard the word "dignity." Pirates walking the plank with sharks circling below act way better than Brian.

I'm looking out the window catching a final glimpse of freedom when we pass Pat Higgins, the village drunk. He waves at us. *Just you wait, Pat*, I think. *Soon enough it'll be your turn to ride back here again.*

We pull into the jail—a loser place with two smelly cells and a kitchen downstairs and quarters for the old jailer and his wife upstairs. Dad shuts off the engine, turns around in the driver's seat and looks us square in the eye. "Stop the blubbering, Brian. Your father wouldn't be pleased."

That clams him up.

"That jail's no fun house, boys. I believe you know that."

"Oh yes, Mister Clancy, yes, I know..."

"Brian, button it and listen to me. Every man deserves a second chance. So if you boys promise never again to do what you did today, I could let you off with a warning."

We promised! Three times!

"And, Brian— you must tell your parents what happened here. Tell them yourself. That's important. I'll be seeing your Dad at the bank tomorrow."

"Yes, Mister Clancy."

And that was the end of it. Just like that. Over and done with. Except in my memory, where it all lives on like yesterday.

Dad loved that little village from the very start, and pretty soon Sherbrooke started warming up to their Mountie. They liked the way he solved crimes and mysteries, like the mystery of the Garden of Eden Ghost. There's this nice old church with an organ and a steeple a few miles outside town in the Garden of Eden—that's really the name of that river valley. The church is in the middle of these hayfields and most of the week, it sits empty. Except on certain moonlit nights when this organ music like from a dream comes floating out across those moonlit fields. Folks are afraid to investigate because they don't want to make the ghost mad; besides, there's that special music you can't hear anyplace else. If you gotta have a ghost, he may as well be talented, right? But of course, the whole spooky thing got reported to Dad, who asked certain people certain questions. A few days later, Dad's at the front door of this old farmer and his wife who have this son still at home and not exactly right in the head. He never went to school but he loves music. Listens to the radio all day and plays this old piano in their living room for his mom and dad at night. Private family concerts right there in the Garden of Eden.

"I believe we need to talk—do we not?"

Everybody says how polite my dad is. These folks invite him right in; they talk. Dad figures out what's going on pretty quick and sees how these folks are afraid of losing their son if they turn him in. Next he talks to the church minister. Then he talks to their son, who Dad says doesn't mean any harm to anybody. Then the Mountie comes up with the solution to the whole thing. Every Sunday from the next week forward, that little congregation listens to the best organist they ever heard! That odd kid living in a world of his own brings that congregation halfway to Heaven just playing the organ at Sunday service. All they had to do was ask him. No more midnight concerts. Church even sets up a midweek Bible study group with him playing organ at the beginning, middle and end. CBC Radio is coming down here to record him next Sunday, that's how good he is. Everybody—the congregation, the minister, the parents of the Garden of Eden Ghost, and the kid himself are all happy—thanks to their Mountie.

Right after solving that one, Dad came up against a problem involving the village hermit. His name's Jack Gabriel, and he has a long white beard and wears blue overalls and lives alone in this log cabin at the edge of town with no electricity or running water. Few folks get to see him, except when he walks into town once a week to get his groceries. But Mr. Gabriel doesn't need people for company because he has his squirrels. The forest by his cabin is full of squirrels, and Mr. Gabriel traps them in this little box that doesn't hurt them. Back home, he has these little wooden cabins waiting for them that he made by hand that look just like his place. Squirrel houses—I'm not kidding. Each has a living room, kitchen and bedroom with a big Red Swan matchbox filled with wood shavings for a bed and his old snuff tins for bowls to eat from. Off the living room is this wire wheel the squirrels hop into and spin around like crazy and get their exercise. Mr. Gabriel calls all his squirrels Jim. Every one. I asked him why and he laughed through his white beard and said, "Because that's their name! They're all Jims."

He's solitary, so people don't really trust Mr. Gabriel. These older kids started tormenting him, driving up to the gravel pit on weekend nights and hollering out at him, even tossing rocks, that kind of thing. He came to our door one day, real upset.

"Those young hooligans come bothering me again, they're going to be ducking buckshot! I'm telling you!" said the hermit.

The Mountie listened. "Thank you for informing me, Mr. Gabriel. Put away your shotgun and let me handle it. Will you do that?"

Then Dad paid a couple of visits to Mr. Gabriel to see how he lived up there. Second visit, he brought me along and said it was OK for me to drop in on him. That's how Jack Gabriel and me became friends.

His cabin was real neat and tidy. He and the Jims were happy and well squared away. He had five Jims living just outside his cabin in tiny houses of their own. One day, I came home from school to find this squirrel house all set up in our front yard! There it was atop a five-foot spruce pole—with a brand-new Jim inside a brand-new house! I peeked into his living room window. Jim hopped out into his wire wheel and took off on the fastest run ever! I swear he was grinning at me—just like Dad, Mom and Mr. Gabriel, who came out of our house where they were watching it all.

That night over dinner, Dad said, "You see, Teller, Jack Gabriel's not such a hermit after all. He's a caring and a generous man."

"What are you going to do about those bad kids?" I said.

"I'm working on it."

And you just knew he was.

Within a week, my Jim would pop out the front door of his house and run a couple of circles around the brim of Dad's big Mountie hat, the two of them grinning like mad. Then one day, Jim started climbing down the pole onto the ground and back up again. Mr. Gabriel told me Jim might even visit his old friends in the forest for a few hours but he'd come back because that house was his home now. But Jim's visits to the forest got longer and longer until one dark day he didn't return home at all. I was really upset: other than Brian Davis, Jim had become my best friend. And the way Brian carried on from time to time, let me tell you I was always glad to come home to Jim and his squirrely grin. Mom explained Jim's disappearance this way: Jim met a nice lady squirrel in the forest, and they decided to go off together and start a family in the woods because there wasn't enough room for a family in that little cabin. That makes sense, doesn't it? Well, as long as Jim's happy that's the main thing. Meanwhile, Dad solved the problem of those young people bothering Mr. Gabriel. He put the word out at Anderson's General Store and Fraser's Garage that Jack Gabriel was a friend of ours, and anybody messing with him would soon find a Mountie knocking on their door. That put a stop to it real quick. Dad told me a smart Mountie doesn't just drive around looking for crimes to solve—he talks to people in advance and heads off trouble that way. Better for everybody, including the bad guys who start thinking twice before doing something they shouldn't.

Come December, Sherbrooke was in the middle of its coldest winter ever. That meant early skating on the pond behind Fraser's Garage.

My friend Paul Sears and I and a bunch of kids were playing pickup hockey when Dad pulled up in the Mountie car. He got out in his fur hat, leather gloves and Mountie boots and came over to the rink. Dad never saw ice skating back in Ireland so he never understood pond ice all that well. Paul and I skated over to him.

"Top of the morning to you, boys! What a day!"

Everybody noticed their Mountie; he waved to the skaters. He loves to watch me play sports. I think he'd be real happy if one day I grew up to be a professional athlete like Ted Williams or Rocket Richard. But this day, all of a sudden there's this *CRACK* sound in the air. My friend Paul says through his green teeth, "The ice is crackin', Micker Clancy, the ice is cracking!" Paul talks funny: "Mister" comes out "Micker." But we don't tease him anymore because his folks have TV, and everybody wants an invite over there to watch.

"Nonsense, Paul! It's just the frost in the air!" says Dad, clapping his leather Mountie gloves together.

Dad's a big man and he dropped through that ice like a stone. As he was going down, he managed to grab onto the top of the boards or he'd have plunged over his head not just up to his armpits. Then he kind of scrambled along the boards, hand over hand like a sea crab —eyes wide as saucers. "Jesus Christ!"

First time I ever heard my dad swear.

Paul and I skated over to the shoreline where Dad stumbled out dripping ice and water and scooted past us towards the police car.

"Don't tell anybody, don't you dare!" he said. Dad was very proud.

"I told him it was cracking! I warned him!" said my green-toothed friend.

"Be quiet, Paul," said I. "Just button it."

Winter gave way to spring, and Sherbrooke Village gave its heart to my father. I could see it in the way they greeted him, in the way they brought vegetables and bottled preserves to our door, in the way they stopped bothering Mr. Gabriel. But I really saw it when Dad returned from a week away in Halifax at an RCMP training course for this fancy new way to catch speeders called radar. Saturday morning, he took me down to Anderson's General Store, where the big men of the village get together to drink coffee and play cards and talk. There was Bob Anderson, who owned the store; Bun Scott, the town barber; Mr. Perkins, our postmaster; Sandy Cameron, the village lawyer; old Magistrate McKeen, who owns Holly Hill Farms; and loopy Pat Higgins with that toothy grin of his getting coffee for all the men. Dad and I walk in, and everybody stops talking. Dad's in uniform.

"What are you fellows staring at?" says the Mountie with the shy smile.

"Welcome back, Dick," says Mr. Anderson.

Grins all around.

"Good to be back. But you boys might not be so happy to see me when I tell you about the magic of radar," says Dad.

Everybody laughed. Oh, they missed him all right.

I don't mean to say everything's been perfect since we moved here; we've had our share of sadness. Last month, we were sitting down to dinner when we hear this screeching of car tires. Up we jump and rush to the window to see this driver beside his car peering at the road in front of his bumper.

"Stay here, Teller," said Dad and went outside.

The driver was picking up my dead dog, Fluffy, by his hind legs. Mom started crying right on the spot, and so did I, even though I'm supposed to be a young man. I'm sorry, it was just too much seeing Fluffy like that. He wasn't a year old, and happy every minute. How can your world change so fast? It's kinda scary if you let yourself think about it. Maybe it's all part of growing up, but that doesn't mean you have to like it.

Ever notice how good news usually follows bad? Like somebody drives over your bike and flattens it—then you hear about this thing called "insurance" and soon you've got a brand-new bike! Soon after Fluffy died Dad got the best news from the RCMP—a promotion from first class constable to corporal! He's been fourteen years a constable so this was a big deal. Non-commissioned-officer stripes and all. Cards and letters from his police buddies and village friends came rolling in. Dad said this means we could be staying in Sherbrooke a good long while—the area's growing, and there's talk of bringing in another constable to help Dad out. But before our celebrations had ended, something really shocking happened: a lady turned up murdered. This is the first time anyone's been killed around Sherbrooke since anybody can remember.

A few days later, Dad arrested the husband of the dead lady and brought him to jail. I saw the man get out of the back of the police car in handcuffs, and he didn't look one bit sorry for his loss. Just angry.

The way he looked at Dad, you'd think Dad was the killer, not him. His own kids wouldn't go visit him in jail. The lady fell down a cliff while she was out hiking. The husband tried to let on he was someplace else but he wasn't—he was with her. Dad was called by her kids when she went missing. He found her lying at the bottom of a cliff on the rocks.

"I can't discuss the particulars," he told Mom and me. "But I've been a Mountie fourteen years—I've seen a lot. And that is a bad man. It's just a matter of proving it."

The trial was being held forty miles away in Antigonish in this big brick courthouse. Dad prepared six weeks, day and night. When the trial began, Dad drove there early every morning and returned after supper.

On the final day of the trial, Dad took me with him. In the courthouse, everyone was dressed up the same way they are at church on Sunday. But the feeling in the room was a whole lot less happy. The man being charged owns this big sawmill and has money. He hired this fancy defense lawyer from Halifax, who gave my father a really hard time on the witness stand. Dad sat there all upright in his red Mountie uniform with the gold stars and buttons on the jacket. The lawyer wore a shiny blue suit with a red tie. The more he told his lies, the more it seemed his tie was stained with the blood of that poor woman.

"Corporal, when you discovered the victim lying on the rocks at the bottom of the cliff, you were alone with her. So isn't it possible that anyone alone with her—including yourself—could have pushed the victim to her death? There were no witnesses, yet for some unknown reason, you have decided to pin this whole incident on her husband. Isn't that true?"

I thought trials in big, fancy courthouses were all about getting to the truth. But this one wasn't—I could tell from Dad's face that he saw it happening, like a car accident he was watching but couldn't prevent.

"Teller, the truth is the last thing that lawyer's interested in," said Dad. "He should be selling fridges to the Eskimos."

The jury's verdict came in: not guilty. Everybody was shocked. Dad took it hard. "That poor woman—I let her down. And her kids," he said.

But trials can go either way, and my father did his very best—this I know. But the whole thing put a sort of cloud over us in Sherbrooke. I could feel that cloud...

—⁂—

Yesterday another surprise came our way. The RCMP told Dad they were transferring him after just a year and a half here.

"It's funny," Dad said. "You get yourself a promotion and you think you're settling down for a good while in a good place—but guess what? The RCMP decides it's time to broaden your horizons again."

He was making a joke, but I felt bad for him. My father had to leave his beautiful home in Ireland because of my grandfather the senator, and now he has to leave this village where we're happy because of that trial. But he's still admired by everybody here. Dad and I went into Anderson's store where Mr. Anderson and the important men around the village were talking. Mr. Anderson said, "Dick, we've had policemen here before, but you're the first real policeman Sherbrooke's known."

I know they won't soon be forgetting Corporal Clancy around here. Mom and I told him so last night. My Dad's the quiet type and doesn't make a big show of his feelings. But last night, he gave Mom and me the biggest hug ever. People around here like their Mountie because they know he's an honest and smart and fair man. And Mom and me— we outright love him, even though we never say that word out loud.

I just have to say one last thing: no jury in some faraway place is ever going to tell me my father was wrong about that case. That will never happen. **I know the Mountie in the house. And I know the truth.**

The End

... of a small town tale.

PUSS 'N' BUTCH

What's in a Name?

They grew up in sixties small-town Nova Scotia—not close friends, but classmates and well enough aware of each other: Don and John. It was the era of nicknames, especially for the guys: Dink, Chink, Trapper, Grey Owl, Fats, Dee Dee, Bird. **Their two nicknames stood out as polar opposites: Puss and Butch.** John assumed his nickname comfortably and unselfconsciously, quite enjoying the swagger implied by "Butch." Don, on the other hand, struggled mightily against his unfortunate tag from the dark day it was bestowed by Sharkey Reid, a smartass classmate living on the next block. Puss wasn't gay, which rendered it all the more infuriating. Tough luck: the nickname stuck.

Why "Puss?" No particular reason. Why "Dink," "Bird," or "Dee Dee"? The nicknames just popped up and assumed a good-natured small-town life of their own. "Puss" was simply unshakeable. Like doggie doo on his Hush Puppies, a cloud of mosquitoes at a summer picnic, a wasp circling cotton candy. Telling people he didn't appreciate the nickname merely heightened its popularity. It was a guaranteed laugh at class parties—as in, "What's new, Pussycat?" shouted across the room. Girls snickered; guys at pickup baseball games picked him last. That Puss was physically uncoordinated, introspective, prone to acne and took violin lessons didn't help. His struggle against the "Puss" image led him to buy a black leather motorcycle jacket. But the tough-guy jacket and the nerdy violin case made an unfortunate comic combination as Puss trudged across town to his lessons. All of which reinforced the growing impression in Puss's mind that the whole town was laughing at him—not entirely true, but true enough to incubate a deep and abiding hatred of this snickering place he was obliged to call home. Butch, on the other hand, sailed in the most average way through school and on to college, propelled by the dream of becoming a police officer charged with upholding the way of life of communities just like this.

Twenty-five years passed. Happily, the two were able to pursue career paths that brought fulfillment and recognition. Butch joined the national police force—the Royal Canadian Mounted Police—and at the twenty-year mark returned to his old hometown. Andy Griffiths returning in triumph to Mayberry. Puss, on the other hand, left town forever straight after high school and didn't stop barreling in the opposite direction until blocked by the blue Pacific. In Vancouver, he developed a successful career as a writer of plays and novels, which he found deeply satisfying since: (1) he chose all the names and nicknames, and (2) as a writer, he meted out reward/punishment/praise/derision to whomever he damn well pleased. He was in charge. Never did he return for a summer vacation, class reunion or nostalgic visit. There was no nostalgia, and after his parents moved away, no reason to drop in. In the past ten years, he had found himself taking a perverse pleasure in turning down invitations to class reunions. His literary assistants fielded the e-mails and phone calls. Puss remained aloof.

"Why would I want to celebrate Asshole High? I already have a full life; they ought to try getting one."

He rejected hometown "friend" requests to his Facebook page. Someone mailed him an obituary of a high school Algebra teacher from the local paper. His assistant handed it to him.

"Smartass old fart. Cruel in the classroom. I doubt death has improved him."

He had a way with words: if he didn't like you, get out of the way.

Two years earlier, he had hired a new assistant, a fresh-faced master of fine arts graduate from a top university creative writing program. Ruth was well-organized, bright, idealistic—she found his literary success and mordant sense of humor appealing. Today, she had yet another high school reunion invite to present. Unlike the others, this one carried special heft.

"Your class has invited you as guest of honor at their 25th reunion in July. Centre of the head table for the class banquet. Listen to a special tribute to your work. Give a speech on a topic of your choosing. Carried on local cable TV. All expenses paid."

"Oh. Oh. The sentimentalists are flocking again. Tell them to flock off."

"A crystal plaque for you to take home and a $10,000 donation to a charity of your choice. The head of the organizing committee will personally bring you to the various events."

"And who might that be?"

The assistant consulted her notes. "Margie Tucker—her maiden name. She said you'd recognize it."

"Oh, yes. I asked her out once," he said flatly.

"Who do they have in mind to give the tribute?"

"Sharkey Reid," she said.

"Hopeless jerk."

"How come?" she said.

"Let's just say he was into nasty nicknames."

He arose from his desk and crossed to the window overlooking Vancouver's English Bay. "OK, here's the deal: they get a different speaker to introduce me, they line up a phone interview with the local rag that must be published with my photograph in advance or I don't get on that plane, my new book will be included in the reunion registration packet, an eight-foot-wide welcome banner will be unfurled behind the head table on my arrival, I will be sent a first-class return air ticket and one economy ticket for you, and they will ensure a certain Mr. Sharkey Reid does not attend the tribute dinner or I will not enter that banquet room. Got all that?"

"Yes, sir."

"One more thing," he said.

Her pen was poised.

"Where is my dry cleaning? Ruth, do you really expect me to attend that network meeting dressed like the janitor?"

She lunged for the phone. "Sorry! I'll take care of it!"

He looked on darkly. "Have you any idea how many eager beavers applied for the position I gave you?"

The day before their departure, his assistant had a rare favor to request.

"I've just completed my first short story," she said.

"How exciting," he said.

"If you don't mind my asking—I was wondering if you might read it on the plane? It won't take long, and I'd be very grateful for any comments or suggestions." Reading and commenting on his drafts was something she regularly did for him, at his request. He paused.

"I'm a playwright and a novelist, Ruth. I don't write short stories. I don't really have a grip on that genre. I don't think I could be very helpful to you."

Her disappointment showed. "Oh—I see..."

"Now here's why I choose not to write short stories: I find them—restrictive. Writing short stories is like trying to shit tiny perfect turds. Not exactly something a novelist aspires to."

A sharp response came to mind, but she wisely stifled it.

Next day, Puss settled into his first-class seat for the long-delayed journey home.

"May I bring you a drink, sir?" said the stewardess.

"Is rock and roll here to stay? Does the Pope wear a funny hat?"

She laughed; he was in top form.

"French champagne, perhaps?" she said.

"You're spoiling me and I love it."

Back in economy, his assistant shrank from the unusually large man strapped in beside her.

"And what do you do for a living?" inquired the stranger.

The guest of honor skipped the pre-dinner events: registration/ welcome dance/pancake breakfast/afternoon barbecue. Four hours before the class dinner, he met with his assistant at his hotel.

"Everything in place per the checklist?" he said.

"Everything," she said.

"The stipulation Sharkey Reid not attend?"

"He wasn't very happy."

Puss smiled.

"One additional item: the town Mountie has offered to provide an official escort to the banquet. Police cruisers front and back, lights flashing, no sirens."

The guest of honor beamed. "You've got to be kidding! A police escort—how thoughtful!"

"The Mountie says you know him—Butch Gray."

"Good old Butch! Well, well—why don't we just take him up on that?"

"All the folks I've talked with are really excited to see you again after all these years," she said.

He leaned back in his armchair. "Funny little town. They'll throw you a tribute dinner, but try getting a prom date…"

His assistant closed her iPad. "Maybe you shouldn't be quite so hard on them. People change, evolve…" she said.

"I'm being hard on THEM? Ha! Hop in my time machine, and I'll whisk you back on a friendly tour of small-town Hell!"

His assistant's smooth brow puckered. "Why did you agree to attend the reunion in the first place?"

"First of all, I'm attending a tribute dinner as guest of honor, not a class reunion. Big difference. Second, bear in mind the trade I ply for a living. Lately, I've been running short on assholes and baddies for the new novel. People you meet these days are so damned polite—so politically correct. My life is one big inoffensive dinner party. I'm suffocating! I need a fresh batch of jerks and quirks for the new book—and guess where I'm gonna find them? This incestuous little anthill of hick-town hypocrites feeding on each other—it's a literary goldmine! Eat your heart out, Stephen King! I'll show you small-town horrors to spare!!"

With that, Puss broke into an unrestrained high-pitched cackle the likes of which his assistant of two and a half years had never heard before.

Twenty minutes before the big dinner, an immaculately uniformed Mountie greeted the writer in the hotel lobby.

"Welcome home, Don," said the Mountie.

He avoided the dreaded nickname; they shook hands.

"You're pretty snappy in red, Butch. Caught any bad guys lately?"

The Mountie chuckled. "Nothing worth writing about. It's a law-abiding little town."

"You bet. A regular Mayberry," said the writer.

The Mountie escorted the guest of honor outside to a brown

Cadillac Seville, where a perfectly coiffed woman in her mid-forties stood waiting.

"Thank you so much for coming, Don. It's wonderful to see you. Welcome home!"

The class president extended her hand in the restrained small-town manner that had never left her. "You're looking very well," she said.

"Better than when I asked you to the prom?" he said.

She laughed. "I know. I missed my big chance to get out of here. But let me try to make it up to you tonight," she said.

They eased into the Cadillac, the police cruisers turned on their lights, and off they went.

Precisely at 8 p.m., they arrived at the 108-year-old curling club and proceeded inside. The guest of honor and class president walked side by side into the dining room, preceded by Mountie Butch Gray and followed by two RCMP constables. Just over 150 classmates, seated at tables for six, rose and broke into applause as they proceeded to the head table where the other class officers were pre-seated. The assembly broke into song:

> *"For he's a jolly good fellow*
> *For he's a jolly good fellow*
> *For he's a jolly good fellow*
> *Which nobody can deny!"*

The guest of honor beamed, shaking outstretched hands as he walked to his place at the head table. He took his seat, the room then sat down and the class president spoke.

"Welcome all, to our 25th class reunion and special tribute dinner.

To introduce our very special guest of honor, I call upon our class historian Robert 'Bird' Fancy."

A pleasant middle-aged schoolteacher rose and took the head table microphone.

"When I was asked to introduce our guest of honor, the first task I faced was what name to introduce him by. The name his parents gave him: Donald Clark? Nobody called him 'Donald.' The name he wrote his first plays under: 'Don' Clark? The name on his first two books: DJ Clark? Or the name on his most recent book: Don MacDonald Clark, MacDonald being his mother's maiden name. Or how about a certain nickname? Remember that one? Oh, no—we won't even go there! Ha! Ha! So of course we asked our guest of honor for guidance on the name question, and guidance he gave us—in writing, of course! Dear classmates, allow me to unfurl the welcome home banner for tonight's guest of honor!"

The class historian gripped a gold cord attached to the large banner behind the guest of honor, pulled it, and it unfurled:

WELCOME HOME, PUSS!!

The room went absolutely stone silent. Then a few female titters. Then a growing laughter. Someone began tapping their spoon against their wine glass. Now the room was laughing uncontrollably and joining in a musical tapping of 150 wine glasses. A spontaneous crowd chant welled up from the banquet floor.

"PUSS! PUSS! PUSS!"

The guest of honor sat impassively. As the chanting and laughter finally subsided, he rose and tapped the microphone before him. It was live.

"Can you hear me?"

The room nodded and murmured vigorously. A comedian piped up from the rear.

"Loud and clear, Puss!"

More laughter. The guest of honor leaned into the microphone. "Then hear this: FUCK YOU ALL! FUCK YOU STRAIGHT UP THE ASS ALL THE WAY TO HELL!"

Thus ended the tribute dinner. Puss returned to his hotel and ordered room service and plenty of booze. The following morning found him massively hungover, meeting with his assistant over breakfast.

"I've had calls from the class president and the entire organizing committee. They're very embarrassed and totally apologetic."

"I couldn't give a pinch of bitter cat shit," he said.

"They want to meet with you," she said.

"They did that last night, remember?" he said.

"They said it was just some prankster."

"Oh really? Who? The class president? The empty suit that introduced me? Sharkey Reid, whom we banned from the dinner? The entire organizing committee? It could have been any of those. You saw them all laughing! Every one of them!"

She tried to reason with him. "They don't take it seriously like you do. For them it's—it's just a silly old nickname, that's all," she said.

"Do me a favor, will you?" he said.

"Of course," she said.

"Just shut up about the matter entirely if you want to go on working for me."

A waiter interrupted. "Mr. Clark, there's someone for you at the front desk."

"Tell them to piss off," said Puss.

"I can't do that, sir," said the waiter.

"Oh, I think you can," said the writer.

"It's the Mountie and he says it's not a social call," said the waiter.

At Butch's suggestion, they met privately in the writer's hotel room.

"So you wanna give me a ticket for public profanity last night? Go ahead, Butch. I could use a good laugh right about now."

The Mountie wasn't joking.

"I need to talk to you about the fire that burned Sharkey Reid's house to the ground last night," said Butch.

"What?" said Puss.

"He barely escaped in his pajamas. Looks like arson. Sharkey's the one who gave you that nickname, right? And didn't you have him banned from last night's dinner?"

Butch's words hung there like dirty laundry on the line.

"Great work, Butch. You went to university, then police academy, then twenty years in the RCMP to come up with crazy shit like this? I'm impressed, Sherlock. Mayberry is in good hands. All I can add is that last night's inferno couldn't have descended on a more deserving asshole. The devil came to claim his own!"

"Very colorful. But this isn't fiction; it's reality. Where were you between 2 and 3 this morning? The front desk says you weren't in your room."

"If I told you, I might get somebody in trouble," said Puss.

"If you don't tell me, you'll be in a lot more trouble yourself," said Butch. "But first, let's back up a little. I have a high school nickname too, remember? Is it such a big deal? Is it worth getting all steamed up about?"

"OK, wanna trade? From now on, I'm Butch, and you're Puss. Mountie Puss. How about it? Everybody including your kids calls you Puss!"

"So what?" said the Mountie. "It's like that Johnny Cash song, *A Boy Named Sue*. His dad gave him that sissy name to make him tough—make him stand up to the kids who teased him."

The writer became visibly angry. "That's a fucking song, Butch! Not real life. How would Johnny Cash have made out if his name was Sue Cash? Hey? Answer that!"

"Here's my answer: if you get this angry with me in a simple conversation, how angry can you get with Sharkey Reid, who tagged you with that nickname?"

"Sorry, Sherlock: your cartoon Q&A is over," said Puss.

"No, it's not. It's just beginning," said Butch. "You're under arrest on suspicion of arson. And you will remain my guest in jail until you tell me your whereabouts last night, and I've been able to verify your alibi. How you liking Mayberry now, sir?"

An hour later, the Mountie was checking out Puss's alibi with the local bootlegger, Stinky Mur, still in business these past thirty years thanks to the restrictive drinking laws of a small town that managed its vices tightly.

"Yeah. He was here all night, Mountie. Real mad, too. Talking about how this small town never changes, how he's going to get them all real good in his next book. But deep down he's a real nice guy, Butch. I remember him from the old days: a real pussycat."

"What time did he leave your place?" said the Mountie.

"Just before 2," said the bootlegger.

"Did he say where he was going? Did he mention Sharkey Reid?"

"Nobody like that. Said he was heading across the street to visit my competition for old time's sake."

The Mountie moved on to the town's second bootlegger, Needle Eye Jones.

"Hey, Butch. I didn't do nothing!"

Needle Eye confirmed that Puss had in fact been at his establishment for a full hour after departing Stinky Mur's.

"Hey—that sonumbitch Stinky trying to get me in trouble, isn't he? Last week he's telling folks I got cockroaches here. Never hear me talkin' trash 'bout him, 'cause roaches only go where there's food! Oh yeah, and see that old wreck in his driveway? Hood always popped open—bill collectors address their bills to him: Stinky Mur, 1969 Chevrolet, Running Springs, Nova Scotia, 'cause they know mailman gonna drop them bills down that engine 'cause Mur's underneath bangin' and clankin', tryin' to start her up and he's gonna be showered with them envelopes. And Stinky's bad-mouthing me? Ha!"

Competitive fires burning brightly, fueling an alibi for a writer.

"Thank you, Needle Eye," said the Mountie.

—⁂—

Later that day, Butch unlocked a jail cell. "Sorry for the inconvenience, but you weren't exactly cooperating."

"That's OK, Butch. You've got a very small town to keep on the rails—right?"

"Yes, I do. I also interrogated Sharkey. He lives alone and is a heavy smoker. Seems your banning him from the banquet bothered him enough that he spent last night home alone with a forty-ouncer of Canadian Club. Probably started the fire accidentally."

Puss smiled. "Gotta love the karma…"

Butch regarded his old classmate closely.

"You're awfully hard on us. Can this place really be all that bad? It produces some talented individuals from time to time—even tries to honor them."

There was a rare slowdown in Puss's swiftly flowing verbal stream. "It's been good seeing you after all these years," said Puss.

"Take it easy on your country cousins," said Butch.

Puss cast him a baleful glance. "Maybe I'll think about that."

"I wish you'd thought about it thirty years ago," said Butch. "The minute you let them get under your skin, you let them know they won the name game. Is a freakin' nickname worth cursing out your class-mates over? And provoking a near-fatal house fire? Get over it, man. Every dog has his day. And every Puss, too. How you handle the yokels is entirely up to you."

"So now I don't just get a Mountie, I get a philosopher. Is that it?"

"Yes, as a matter of fact, it is. Look, give your nickname a chance, man! It's a great handle for somebody in the public eye like yourself. I mean, Puss is right up there with Alice Cooper and Johnny Rotten and Meatloaf and The Animals!"

"Excuuuse me if I'm not interested in being a feminized version of a rotten meatloaf!"

"Funny as always, but you're missing the point, man. Careers are built on names. Puss may have dragged you down in high school, but it's a hell of a *nom de plume*! Remember The Sopranos? It was just the most popular series in HBO history. Remember the Mafia don who was feared and respected by all the bad guys and their ladies? His name: Big Pussy! The name was so powerful it was adopted by his lieutenant, Little Pussy. Doesn't that tell you something, Puss? Like The Beatles say in *Hey Jude*: 'Take a sad song and make it better.' It's all up to you, man! Stop living in the past and make it work for you."

—∞—

A week later the writer and his assistant were back in the sunny office overlooking Vancouver's English Bay.

"Twenty-seven letters from your classmates have come in apologizing for what happened," said his assistant.

"Shred 'em. Every one of those two-faced pricks was laughing at the time. But send Sharkey Reid a note—say we heard his house burned down—recommend he get a fire alarm in his next place and some fireproof PJs while he's at it! Good ole Sharkey! Doing the hotfoot hip-hop!"

Again, the high-pitched cackle rang out. His assistant looked up from her notes.

"I wonder who could have done the banner thing…"

"Oh, that's easy!" said Puss. "Sharkey, of course. Pissed off we banned him from the dinner. Switched banners at the printers. Only to return home to the inferno from Hell. *Love* those small towns! You can't invent plots like that!"

The writer was hugely amused.

The assistant closed her memo pad. "Is there anything else?" she asked.

"Word factory closed for the day. How's your short story coming along?"

"Fine, thank you. I'm taking my work in a more realistic direction," she said.

"Keep plugging away. Sorry I can't be more help. Don't have a real grip on that genre."

"I understand," she said.

"I knew you would," he said.

Later that evening while the writer dined alone at his private club, his assistant, Ruth, opened her mail in her modest apartment. There it was:

ZENITH PRINTERS:

One eight-foot PUSS vinyl color banner: $200.

Somewhere deep in the heart of the throbbing heart of the city, a lone long-suffering literary assistant smiled demurely to herself.

The End

... of the nickname from Hell.

A SEASIDE ROMANCE OR TWO

Chivalry in New Jerusalem

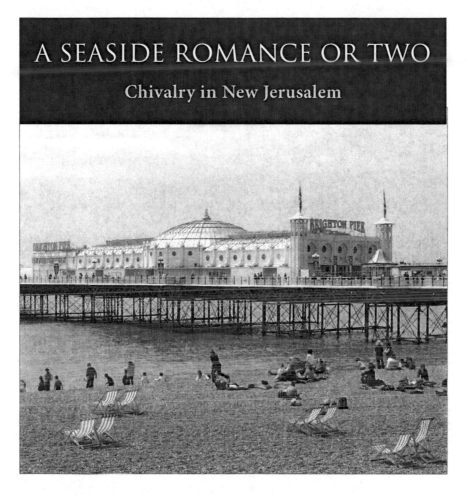

Teller arrived in England from Canada to read politics at Sussex University in Brighton and immerse himself in a culture he had admired from afar; the birthplace of ancient chivalry, Beatlemania, and the rich language he spoke and wrote. Now the short train ride from Heathrow to Victoria Station, change to British Rail's Brighton Belle, clattering down to the seaside town, a swift sixty miles south of London on the English Channel. He took a small apartment in Regency Square just down from the Palace Pier, from a gentleman with the quintessential English name Nigel Lemon. Soon there was a pub he liked: the equally English *King and Queen* on Grand Parade. It was traditional, large, convivial, and the draught lager was cheap—a sterling set of attributes for a student on a budget. It became his "local" and it was there he met Liverpool Larry, who brought him to Grace and Gordon.

Larry had a direct link to British pop royalty: he grew up on the same block as John Lennon. Larry claimed the great Lennon himself broke his nose, giving it the distinctive crook he was clearly proud of.

"I told him Little Richard was just a flaming faggot. That's all it took, man. *Blam!* Right in the old snot catcher! You figure it's too late to sue the bastard?"

"Let me buy you a drink," replied Teller.

"Ta, mate! Make it a Newcastle Brown. But I'm reserving me legal rights against Lennon. I used to be movie star 'andsome, you know?" Liverpool Larry and his shaggy pals with the nasal twangs laughed.

"When's the last time you saw the great Beatle?" Teller asked.

"Six months ago. Ran into him on the old street—visiting his Aunt Mimi, he was. I said ''Ow's it going, Johnnie?'"

"'Orrible, Larry,' he says. 'Bloody awful! Got a hernia last week lugging me loot to Barclays!'"

More laughter. It felt like an impromptu Beatles press conference: great fun.

"Last round, ladies and gentlemen, if you please! Final round!"

England's un-festive 11 p.m. closing time was upon them. No bother: Liverpool Larry had a plan.

"Right, lads: apple cider—two quarts each. Load up! Opening hour at Grace and Gordon's!"

He turned to the student from Sussex.

"Party time! And you're in the entourage!"

Liverpool Larry led the way on foot up Western Road, past the Clock Tower where the young Virgin Records had just opened their first store outside London, on past Regency Square, to Montpelier Place and up the hill to the last building on the left. A small grocery occupied the main floor, apartments above, and ten steps below sidewalk level a small patio, potted plants, and the doorbell Larry was ringing.

"Larry, me old lad! What a lovely surprise!" said a ruddy, ponytailed man in his early forties.

"Top of the evening to you, Gordon. I brought a new friend."

Inside, a party was in full swing. Their hosts were Grace and Gordon—a childless forty-something Cockney couple with a love of homemade wine, rock music, late nights, and young people. Gordon resembled Michael Douglas, except for the Cockney accent and ponytail secured by a rubber band. Grace was a petite, strikingly beautiful former ballerina with jet black hair, flawlessly applied makeup and a slight tummy brought on by the steady flow of wine over the years. They had the easy gift of treating everyone like visiting royalty. Their one-bedroom basement apartment with the perpetually glowing coal fireplace and beautifully upholstered antique furniture was a social salon frequented by an engaging collection of Brighton eccentrics. There was Spud and Barbara, inseparable from each other and whatever intoxicant was on the go; Mick the Spiv, who always sported a suit and top hat; Sketchy Gilbert, who could dash off a fine charcoal likeness in five effortless minutes; Somerset Peter, who painted impressionist oils and carried amazing weed; Jen and Pat, the hopelessly in love deaf and dumb couple with remarkably animated faces; Alfie the Cockney con man, best friend to everyone but "the fuzz;" Supercilious Sal who could never be taken at face value; Professor Ted, the Sussex lecturer who lived for chess; Bubbly Mary with husband Brian, who, to Mary's bemusement, held court quite nude before the fireplace while Grace remarked: "Oh, Brian, you are silly!"

And on it went...

Since he liked the vibe, and since a warm welcome now awaited him a ten-minute walk from home, he dropped in frequently. They grew comfortable in each other's company. Grace and Gordon, though never married, had been together fifteen years. Grace's agoraphobia— her fear of open spaces—had forced her to leave the corps de ballet at Sadler's Wells. Gordon's trade as a master upholsterer supported them. They had departed hectic inner London for the more tranquil environs of seaside Brighton. Grace could make occasional excursions outside the apartment on Montpelier Place, although never as far as Paris, which Gordon had longed to visit with her for many years.

They did go pubbing, with Gordon wearing a suit jacket and clerical collar and Grace proclaiming every evening out as her birthday. The Vicar and the Birthday Lady rarely paid for a drink and never lacked for company in the many pubs of Brighton. Introduced as their visiting nephew from The Colonies, their new friend was included in the festivities.

Gordon spoke of a childhood spent outside London for safety during the war, watching British Spitfires duel with German Messerschmitts high above waving fields of rye.

"Those lads were true heroes, weren't they? Where have all the heroes gone? Become bus drivers and tax collectors, it seems," he said.

"Aren't you being a bit hard on jolly old England, Gordon?" asked Teller.

"Am I? It seems today's heroes are either rock stars or comic book heroes. Hardly the caliber of our heroes during the war."

"Oh, Gordon, do shut up! Stop being so bleedin' morose. Life is bloody marvelous. If you can't bubble and bath, then keep quiet," said Grace.

"Yes, my trouble and strife."

They were using Cockney rhyming slang; it was confusing.

"Gordon, the poor boy is baffled!"

"Trouble and strife means wife," Gordon said. "She wants me to shut up if I can't bubble and bath—laugh. Cockney rhyming slang."

"Very cool," said Teller.

"Time to move these plates of meat," said Grace, rising from the table.

"Plates of meat—feet," whispered Gordon conspiratorially.

Music filled the pub, drawing Grace to the dance floor where she did an entrancing ballet solo. Applause filled the room. Her escort, the vicar-for-a-night, looked on beaming.

"Do you believe it? She's like April showers, bloomin' 24-7..."

"Sunshine on a cloudy day, Gordon," said their young friend.

"Exactly right, me old china plate. I'm well aware, mate."

Apart from parties and young people, Grace and Gordon shared a deep and abiding interest in nature. The couple brought Teller to one of their favorite Brighton spots, an herb garden for the blind. Here grew some forty herbs, on the other side of a brass railing where braille plaques named the plants. Every second Sunday, their Brighton salon would congregate at the Clock Tower bus stop and board the Number 52 for the countryside. Forty minutes later, they disembarked at a rural bus stop, and made their way to their secret campsite in the woods where they gathered bags of elderberries for Grace's elderberry wine. Dusk found them around the campfire for stories and song until the last bus departed for Brighton. There the party continued at Grace and Gordon's until two or three in the morning.

Come spring, Gordon accepted an upholstering job "in situ," which he explained was the term for working at a client's home. Every day, Gordon would don a jacket, shirt and tie and walk to the large Georgian apartment in Bedford Square—the home of Mrs. Crenshaw. He had been recommended by an antique dealer and accepted an assignment to re-cover her large and valuable antique living room set.

Mrs. Crenshaw was an attractive fifty-ish widow with a fine figure and wide-set blue eyes. Middle-age marvelous, as Gordon put it. She had been left by her husband with time and money on her hands. He was a stockbroker in the City, one of Brighton's Bowler Hat Brigade who made the daily one-hour commute to London aboard the Brighton Belle. He was the epitome of moderation, exercise and physical fitness— all the healthy habits Gordon avoided. No matter—one Wednesday, the

Belle returned Mr. Crenshaw to Brighton in his private compartment quite dead, thanks to a congenital heart defect. Six months later, his widow was getting her furniture refinished and, thanks to Gordon, her interest in life renewed. He had the gift of lively conversation joined to a sweet nature: two qualities Mrs. Crenshaw's late husband lacked. Gordon's innate refinement and effortless sociability were appreciated by the lady. And her charms were not lost on him.

"She's a proper lady—to the manor born. Offers me a gold watch—Scotch!—promptly on arrival. And I must say has the most beguiling mince pies—eyes!"

"Really, Gordon? Have you told her so?" asked his Canadian friend.

"Perish the thought! This is Olde England, chum. Professional distance and all that," said Gordon.

When Mrs. Crenshaw discovered Gordon's interest in nature, she asked him to assist in the care of her large walled garden. In this special place, Gordon was transported to a higher plane.

"It is truly heavenly. No other term for it, mate. It's like this: assume you live a good life, die honorably, and proceed straight to Heaven; you will be greeted by dear old St. Peter at the Pearly Gates. Right? Right. This timeless gent will check your tally in the Book of Life, find you worthy, I am sure, then swing open those Heavenly Gates, and usher you into—Mrs. Crenshaw's English garden! That, my young friend, best describes this place of intense beauty. I am truly blessed each day, just to enter there." A social class divide beautifully bridged.

One fall day, Mrs. Crenshaw's tailor arrived to take Gordon's measurements. Four days later, the gentleman returned with a gardening jacket of the finest Harris Tweed and a pair of deerskin gloves for trimming the rose bushes. Gordon and Mrs. C, as he now called her, were taking lunch daily on her second-floor patio overlooking the sea. This is where Mick the Spiv spotted them as he ambled past along the seafront promenade.

"Hello, Gordon!" jaunty Mick called out, doffing his trademark top hat.

Gordon smiled and waved.

"Who is that amusing fellow?" asked Mrs. Crenshaw.

"An old pal," he said.

"Shall we invite him up?"

"Time I got back to work," replied Gordon.

Mick the Spiv carried on, whistling and receding into the distance.

And this is how news of Gordon's seaside lunches reached Grace—from Mick the Spiv to Supercilious Sal at Saturday's party, to Grace.

"So this is why I haven't had to prepare your lunch lately, Gordon. How nice for the two of us," said Grace.

"It's steady bread and honey," said Gordon.

"What kind of honey? Mick says she has a right nice set of Bristol cities."

Gordon blushed.

"Why, look everyone—our Gordon's blushing! Got a fancy lady—has our Gordon! Cheeky monkey! Getting a bit on the side, are we?"

He was not. Grace's laughter dissolved into an uncontrolled coughing fit.

"Easy, my darling," said Gordon, placing an arm around Grace's petite shoulders.

"No—you take it easy, Romeo! Just bugger off! Don't strain your whatsit!" More hacking laughter from Grace. A chill breeze thanks to Mick the Spiv.

Come Monday, Gordon arrived at work to music: Mrs. Crenshaw had *The King and I* on the stereo. A buoyant young woman's voice filled the living room: *"Getting to know you, getting to know all about you..."*

"It's lovely," he said with a smile.

"I'm happy you like it," she said softly.

Their eyes met; away from a party, Gordon was a shy man. He averted his eyes from the lady's gaze.

Vicar Gordon and Birthday Lady Grace continued their rounds of the pubs of Brighton. It was common for Gordon in his clerical collar to be approached by troubled souls seeking spiritual and personal counsel. Two such encounters took place at the Brighton House in the famous Lanes area. A comely young woman approached their table asking for a private moment with the Vicar. Gordon excused himself.

"Vicar, I have sinned and cannot stop."

"How, my girl?" Gordon asked.

"I have been married two years. But these past five months, I have been unfaithful to my husband," she said.

"Unfaithful? With whom?"

"The Prince of Wales," she responded.

"Charles?"

She nodded solemnly, commanding the Vicar's absolute and total attention.

"Can this truly be?" asked Gordon incredulously.

"Well, with his official portrait, actually—that hangs in our sitting room. While my husband is at work, I recline on the large sofa and pleasure myself while gazing up at His Royal Highness in full ceremonial uniform. I am so ashamed."

"Do you also have normal relations with your husband?"

"Not since this affair began." she said.

"In other words, my dear, might we say you prefer the Prince of Wales' portrait to the actual presence of your husband?"

She was embarrassed by the reality of it all.

"Yes, Father."

"Where is your husband this evening?"

"At home watching telly," she said.

The Vicar had heard enough. "Right. This is a hopeless situation that will not improve. It comes from deep within. Leave your husband. Find a new man more suited to your needs. An officer in the military, I suggest."

"Thank you so much, Vicar! I have had such thoughts myself but lacked the courage to act."

"God bless and keep you, my child," said Gordon.

The second soul to seek counseling was a middle-aged man alone at the bar. "Where is your church, Vicar?"

"My ministry is here, my son. In the pubs and in the streets of Brighton, among God's children."

A fine answer.

"I have broken the law of God and of man," said the total stranger.

"What exactly have you done?"

Embarrassed silence.

"God has heard it all, my son. Unburden yourself," said Gordon.

"I embezzled 17,500 pounds from my employer."

Gordon was unfazed.

"And what have you done with this money?"

"Placed it in the bank."

"Have you been spending it?" asked Gordon.

"No, Vicar," said the thief.

"This is a senseless crime—a sin of extreme selfishness and self-centeredness in the eyes of God."

"Yes, Father."

"You must work immediately at being generous towards others. You may begin by ordering me a double Glenfiddich on the rocks."

The sinner obliged. Gordon took an appreciative sip.

"Next, you must return this money."

"Yes, Vicar—with an apology?"

"Are you absolutely and totally daft? Return it anonymously, unless you prefer saying your prayers in the slammer."

"That I will, God have mercy on me."

Gordon looked at the man appraisingly. "You have the look of a solitary man."

"Yes, Father, I live alone."

"Go to the Brighton animal shelter. Adopt the two ugliest caged creatures you find there—perhaps ones with an eye or limb missing. Save their lives. Bring them home. Be generous."

"My landlord does not permit pets."

"Then you must find a new apartment. Give in your notice tomorrow. Do not hesitate."

The man smiled for the first time in weeks. "Yes, Vicar. The very prospect is most pleasing. Thank you so much."

"And God bless you for the Glenfiddich, my son. Now kindly send two doubles to my wife and her young friend at the adjoining table. Tonight happens to be her birthday. Isn't she lovely?"

Grace was drinking more and enjoying it less. On the way home from the pub she vented. "What kind of vicar are you? With a fancy lady with big Bristol cities on the side? I'm reporting you to the Church of England, mate!" Her braying laughter caught the attention of a strolling bobby.

"Pardon me, Madame. But it is now 11:30 in the PM. Could you kindly lower the volume?"

"What's this, then? An old fart in a policeman's whistle and flute!?" said Grace loudly.

"I do not believe you are paying attention to me, Madame."

"You got that bloody right, mate! Is this all you have to do, bother decent citizens on their way home? Why aren't you out catching bleedin' criminals? Tell me that, then. WHY BLOODY NOT?"

Her friends laughed; Gordon smiled uneasily. The policeman put a hand in his tunic pocket and withdrew a notebook. "Madame, if you persist in this provocative behavior, I shall be forced to take down your particulars." He unsheathed his pen ominously.

"Take down my particulars? Right here on Western Road? Ooooh! Aren't you the naughty boy! Shouldn't we at least duck into an alley?"

Gordon hailed a taxi and, with the assistance of friends, bundled Grace away home.

In addition to the upholstery and gardening, Gordon was now riding with Mrs. Crenshaw in her Jaguar to the finest local nurseries. Gordon's knowledge of flora and fauna was encyclopedic, his recommendations inspired, and Mrs. Crenshaw's English garden grew more beautiful by the week. A green and pleasant place in the heart of the seaside town. Gordon brought her to the herb garden for the blind, which she had never visited. Conversation flowed easily between the couple; Gordon's blithe spirit was warming the widow's lonely heart and reawakening her love of life.

One foggy morning, Gordon picked up his dog and bone to receive a surprise call from Mrs. Crenshaw's lawyer. The gentleman requested a meeting that day at his office.

Tea was served in the lawyer's oak-paneled boardroom with a commanding view of the Brighton Pavilion.

"I am very pleased to make your acquaintance, Mr. West, having heard so many fine things about you."

"Why thank you, guv'nor," Gordon said. "Do you have the need of some upholstery, then?"

The lawyer, entirely lawyerly in pinstripes and reading half-glasses, chuckled benignly. "Another matter brings us together today." The lawyer removed his glasses in a practiced motion. "May I speak personally for a moment?"

"Certainly, guv'nor," said Gordon.

"I understand that you and Mrs. Crenshaw get along well, and in fact have become—may we say—good friends over the past several months."

"Yes, indeed, squire. She is a lovely person."

"Having been in her service over ten years now, I could not agree more. And I hope you are aware that Mrs. Crenshaw thinks very highly of you. She is a cautious woman, and not someone easily impressed."

"A wise way to proceed, in this age of uncertainty," said Gordon.

"Now Mr. West," said the lawyer, "I do not mean to pry, but it is my understanding that, legally speaking, you are a single man. Is this correct?"

"It is."

The lawyer seemed pleased. "Sir, I am here today to present an offer for your consideration. It is not the sort of offer one receives—or indeed makes—every day. And it is definitely an offer that, if accepted, would utterly change your life. I understand you have long harbored a desire to visit Paris? We certainly do not expect a response today. Next week will be fine."

—∞—

Next evening, Gordon was having a rare pint at the pub without Grace. Across the table sat his student friend.

"She proposed marriage through her lawyer?"

Gordon nodded.

"That's incredible, Gordon! What are you going to tell him—I mean—her?"

"I already have. Phoned the gent today," said Gordon. "No sense dragging it out. I can't leave Gracie. That's just not on."

"Have you told Grace about all this?"

"Are you mad? If I opened me big gob, she'd shove me out the door! When Gracie gets down on herself, she's always saying how nutters I am to stay with her. If she knew about this, she'd lock me out and insist I accept! Grace is all about doing for others, never for herself. That's how Gracie lives her life, me old china plate."

The entire extraordinary situation sank in.

—⚭—

Twenty years passed, as did Grace in the twentieth year—peacefully at Brighton General, with Gordon by her side. Gordon wrote his Sussex University friend Teller from long ago, now a screenwriter in Los Angeles. A week later, a courier packet arrived at Gordon's Brighton apartment with a two-week British Airways return ticket from Heathrow to LAX. Gordon arrived, remarkably unchanged. He was now 62, on his first trip outside England: his first palm tree, first surfer, first freeway, first roadside taco truck.

"What on Earth is that?" asked the man most English.

"It's a taco truck, Gordon. Like the chip wagons in England. Only they serve Mexican food."

"Blimey!" said Gordon. "And do they drive up from the Mexican border every morning?"

Over the next two weeks, they caught up with each other's lives while walking the Venice and Santa Monica boardwalks.

"Whatever happened to Mrs. Crenshaw?"

"Mick the Spiv scooped her up. She married him against her lawyer's best advice. They're happy as clams; he's better-dressed than ever, and she's still trying to tame him."

"Liverpool Larry and all the others?"

"Moved back to Liverpool—a tour guide at Lennon's old home; Spud and Barbara—poor old Spud got into the heroin and passed away; Cockney Alfie opened a second-hand shop in the Lanes; Somerset Peter is a society painter now if you please, doing portraits for Mrs. Crenshaw's friends, Professor Ted still comes by for the occasional game of chess…"

"Your wonderful parties? Still going strong?"

"Oh, no, mate. That crowd drifted away after Gracie passed. It seems I'm not quite the host she was…"

They watched the sun go down over Santa Monica Bay. Teller spoke. "You once wondered where all the heroes had gone—those pilots from the Battle of Britain you watched dueling in the sky as a boy," he said.

"Blimey. You remember that? I can tell you where the heroes have gone," said Gordon. "And it's not glamorous. Gone on to become shop clerks and tax collectors. Not England's finest hour, these present times."

Teller looked appraisingly at his old friend most English. "I still think you're a bit hard on that ancient island of yours. Far as I can see, it's still Blake's Jerusalem—that green and pleasant land peopled by everyday heroes. In fact, there's one standing before me right now. The way you stood by Gracie: downright heroic."

Gordon was taken aback. He smiled self-consciously. "Ta, mate. But you've got it backwards. If there's a hero in all this, it's not myself. It was Gracie. Carrying on with smiles and right royal greetings down through the decades, all the while struggling with that illness of hers. That woman gave me love and laughter and a circle of marvelous friends—a life, mate. Gracie gave me a beautiful life."

"Two heroes then, Gordon. Not just one."

The End

... of a very English romance.

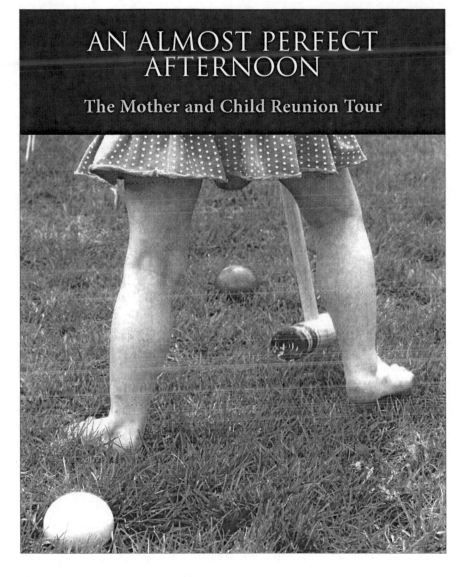

AN ALMOST PERFECT AFTERNOON

The Mother and Child Reunion Tour

I t was the summer of his eleventh year. At the far end of the twelve-hundred-mile drive from his small-town Nova Scotia home, Toronto loomed up over the dashboard of the '54 Pontiac as a shimmering, endless metropolis. The boy loved it. Years later, viewed in hindsight from Manhattan, Toronto appeared the self-satisfied backwater it then was. But that summer, the city was utterly intoxicating; each day promised high adventure.

It was the city of his mother's youth, her twenties and his birth. They had returned after an eleven-year absence to present him to her many old friends and, of course, to stay with Grandma. Dad did not make the journey. Grandma found Dad impatient, while Dad found Grandma selfish. Theirs was an undeclared, deeply felt Cold War with no truce in sight—which left Dad mowing the lawn in Nova Scotia.

Mom, attractive, tall and slim, arranged their visits by phone from a lengthy typed list. It ranged from her elderly and distinguished former boss, the president of General Foods, to numerous female and male friends and colleagues, whom Mom referred to as "guys" and "gals." Toronto seemed to elicit a jaunty new vocabulary from Mom. He liked it.

At the top of their first week's visits were the Kirkbys—the small white-haired Scots couple who were the superintendents of Mom's apartment building while Dad was courting her. For the past eleven years, a bright package from the Kirkbys with his name on it had faithfully appeared under the family Christmas tree. The Kirkbys seemed to lack first names. What they did have was a budgie named Jim, stacks of homemade oatmeal cookies and matching lilting accents. The Maritimes visitors had a fine talkative visit during which the Kirkbys made a great fuss over him, while Mom beamed proudly. The boy was sorry when it ended.

"When will we see the Kirkbys again?" he asked as they pulled away onto Avenue Road.

"On our next trip," replied Mom wistfully.

Day Five's luncheon appointment was special. This old friend had been Number One on Mom's typed list and would have been first on their schedule, except Number One had been "otherwise engaged" the past four days. When the boy asked Mom what she was otherwise engaged in, it was left a mystery. No matter. Mom was now navigating the maroon Pontiac through the leafy streets of Toronto's most exclusive neighborhood, onto the semi-circular driveway of the largest, finest home he had ever seen. Mom had explained that her old friend had "married well." Now Mom was nervously clearing her throat and pressing an illuminated doorbell. The door was instantly flung open as if someone were waiting on the other side, hand on the handle. In fact, someone was.

"Dorothy, you haven't aged a minute! No—make that a second!"

Before Mom could respond, a stylishly dressed thirty-something woman enveloped her and the boy in a huge hug and wrestled them into the foyer. The boy noticed on their hostess the sort of makeup his mother wore when his parents went partying or dancing. It seemed out of place in the afternoon.

"Come in! Come in, you two! Come in!" she said.

The boy inhaled the sweet, pungent aroma of her perfume, which a decade later he would identify as Beefeater Gin.

They occupied three of twelve chairs in the oak-paneled dining room. She served a salad with huge shrimp that reminded the boy of the drumsticks from his small-town Kentucky Fried Chicken. His attention shifted from the shrimp on his plate to the lady's impeccably plucked eyebrows, which were twitching randomly.

"So what on Earth have you been up to all these years, Dorothy—since you abandoned us all for the boondocks?"

Mom smiled. "Being a Mountie's wife—raising a family—growing a garden—writing letters you never responded to—nothing Earth-shattering, really."

"Listen to her! Your mom's a real card—oughta be dealt with!"

Number One burst into raucous laughter—which suddenly stopped.

"Is that an echo or did somebody just enter laughing?"

More raucous laughter. "Just kidding! Ready for the grand tour?"

Martini in hand, she led them through the 16-room mansion, starting with the great, glittering kitchen.

"What gorgeous tile—such detail—such color!"

Mom, who had recently arranged for Sears to install a new Formica countertop, was plainly dazzled.

"Not bad for a girl from the office, right? I must say George is quite quick with the old checkbook. Downright handy that way."

"Lucky you," said Mom.

"I'm the luckiest girl in all of Toronto—just ask George—if you can find him!"

The eyebrows twitched in emphasis. Mom broke the awkward silence. "It's such a large house. Do you have staff?"

"*Moi!* I am the staff! George says he wants me all to himself. Truth is, Georgie's an efficiency nut. Loves spending money on things—hates spending on labor. Secret of his success."

"Do you have pets?" asked the boy. "We've got a dog and a cat. Dad's taking care of them."

"Lucky you with the Mountie dad. George is allergic."

"I hope we have the opportunity to meet George. I left for the Maritimes before he came into your life," said Mom.

"Poor George! Everybody's disappearing on him!" said her old friend.

More raucous laughter. Her statement made no sense to the boy. If anyone had disappeared, surely it was George. Who else could be disappearing from the beautiful house?

"Golf, anyone?" said Number One.

They stood in the half-acre backyard, contemplating an elevated putting green with a fluttering flag atop the hole proclaiming 19. A lone gardener in a green uniform tended the shrubbery on the far side.

"Shouldn't the flag say Number 1?" the boy asked.

"Of course it should! Unless you're George and you're determined to be amusing. 19th hole and all that—where the best post-game parties are."

"If you don't mind my asking, what line of business is George in?"

Mom did not normally ask personal questions. The boy paid attention.

"Munitions." Followed by a pause.

"What are munitions?" asked the boy.

The lady of the house looked down at him through warm watery eyes. "Sort of like fireworks. Only quite a bit louder."

"Sounds like a lot of fun," responded the boy.

"Oh, that depends on where you're watching them from," replied their hostess.

"Do you set them off back here in the backyard?" the boy pursued.

"Actually, no. George sells them to the Americans, and they set them off," said Number One.

"Where?" said the boy.

"All over the world," said Number One.

The tour resumed. They were climbing a massive semi-circular stairway topped by a Tiffany skylight. Near the top, Number One lost her balance and reached out to the wall for support.

"Stormy weather ahead! All hands on deck! All hands on deck!"

More raucous laughter.

"Careful, Elaine! You could lose your balance." Mom looked concerned.

"Ssssssh!! Don't you worry about good old Elaine! Practice and training! That's the key! Plenty of practice! Yo ho ho and a bottle of rum!"

They reached the top of the stairway.

"What a gorgeous skylight!" said Mom.

"It's from Paris at the turn of the century. George has a thing for France—*suivez-moi!* In case they don't teach you that in grade school—it means "follow me!""

The boy liked her. She ushered them through the first of six large doors off the upstairs hallway.

"*Voilà!*"

They were in an imposing wood-paneled office, anchored by a massive carved walnut desk positioned in front of a cut glass window overlooking the 19th hole.

"It was Napoleon's desk. George has the papers to prove it."

"My, my," exclaimed Mom.

"No, Dorothy—his, his." Again, the laugh.

"Where on Earth did he find it?"

"Somewhere or other. George has a way of acquiring whatever he wants."

"Mom—look!"

The boy's attention was captured by a large table that supported an armored battalion of toy soldiers in red uniforms advancing across a heavily fortified nineteenth-century landscape. A general on a white steed led the way.

"He plots their moves from Napoleon's desk, then has me rearrange the pieces as he changes strategy."

"Wow!"

She looked at the boy. "I'm sure it would be more fun for George to play with you."

"Really? When does he get home?"

The ladies laughed uneasily.

Twenty minutes later, grand tour completed, they reassembled on the back patio for gin and tonic.

"Just a light one. I'm driving."

"Don't you worry! No Mounties in this neighborhood!"

Mom smiled. Her old friend looked at her appraisingly.

"All right, Dorothy. So what time does this Mountie of yours get home at night?"

"Five o'clock. On the button. And noon till one every day for his lunch and a nap," said Mom.

"No! You're joking!"

"Not at all. That's our routine."

The lady of the house paused.

"Nap, you say? What kind of nap?"

Mischievous grins flashed between the old girlfriends. They laughed. Innocently, the boy joined in, which heightened their girlish laughter. The summer sun shone benignly on the patio and its occupants. An almost perfect afternoon.

"Excuse me. Would it be OK if I went back upstairs and played with the soldiers a little while?" said the boy.

"Of course," their hostess replied.

The words came out *of coursh*.

"Just promise you'll put the soldiersh back exactly where you found them."

"Promise!" Up the stairwell he bounded.

The boy sat behind Napoleon's desk, feet dangling over the parquet floor. Spread before him on the intricately inlaid desktop were sheets of heavy paper with detailed battlefield drawings. Staring back at him from a photograph in a large silver frame was the master of the house in a Napoleonic general's uniform, accompanied by Mom's old friend dressed as Marie Antoinette. Costumed couples danced in the background. A sword and scabbard hanging on the nearest wall caught the boy's attention. He rose from the general's desk, removed the sword and began slashing the air. "Hah! Hah! Get back! Back, you scurvy devils!"

The dialogue, though lifted from a recent pirate movie, seemed to fit. Sword in hand, the boy strutted imperiously over to the battlefield table and stood peering down at the troops. "Men of France, listen to me! Fight for the glory of France! For the honor of your fathers and families. To return in victory to the towns and villages of your birth! Men of France—*Suivez-moi!* Follow me!"

Atop an imaginary steed, the boy charged around the large study, brandishing his sword overhead. He galloped to the window overlooking the backyard and peered into the middle distance.

"Enemy troops approaching! Attack, men of France, attack!"

He motioned an invisible wave of soldiers forward, then galloped back to the table.

"Reinforcements, mount up! Forward at the gallop!"

He led his reinforcements to the scene of battle.

"Charge! Charge!" he shouted, directing them onwards to the 19th hole.

His commanding efforts produced a sudden thirst, which he combated with a glass of water in the study's marble bathroom. As he sipped, he noticed a small handle in the paneled wall opposite the sink. Idly, he pressed the handle; a hidden door swung silently open.

The boy entered a young girl's hidden bedroom, warmly lit by afternoon sunlight. His eyes widened. To the right, a frilly single bed with pillows decorated with cartoon characters. To the left, a five-foot-high playhouse with a front door, windows and miniature furnishings, an exact replica of the mansion he had been in these past several hours. He turned and opened a closet door; an overhead light came on automatically, displaying hanging coats and dresses sized for a four- or five-year-old. A tall armoire blocked the main door to the bedroom, preventing normal entry and exit. The small hidden doorway he had entered from the general's bathroom seemed the only functioning entrance. He crossed the room to the bedside table and opened a mother-of-pearl encrusted box. A recording issued forth:

Here comes Peter Cottontail

Hopping down the bunny trail...

The room felt like the ghost ships he had read about in pirate yarns—sailing the open ocean, sails unfurled, tea kettle whistling on the galley stove, neither captain nor crew in sight...

The maroon Pontiac rolled back down the cobblestone driveway to the leafy street and freedom.

"But, Mom, we didn't even say goodbye!" He was agitated.

"Yes, I know. Elaine was very tired. Sometimes rest is the most important thing."

"Mom—she passed out in her armchair!"

"Oh, Elaine was just tired," said Mom.

"She was drunk. And I'm telling you—they have a daughter! They really do. Why didn't she say anything?"

"Impossible. They must have prepared that room for a young niece or cousin coming to visit. People of means do that sort of thing."

"I'm telling you, Mom—a little girl around kindergarten age lives in that room. It's no guest room. When's the last time you saw your friend?"

"Oh, it's been years. Did you see any photographs of this—ghostly presence?"

The boy paused. "No—but I could feel her there! Ask your friend to invite us back. Visit the little girl's room for yourself."

But there was no return invitation, despite Mom's prompt thank-you note and cordial phone call. There was, however, a return engagement with the Kirkbys—but the oatmeal cookies and Jim the budgie fared rather poorly against Napoleon's soldiers and battle strategies.

—∞—

Mid-August found Mom and the boy back in Nova Scotia in the modest house on the hill where the Mountie was waiting. Three weeks later, the boy returned from school to learn Mom had news of her old friend in the big house.

"She wants us to come back and meet her husband and little girl? They're all coming down here for a visit? What's happening?"

The boy was excited.

"I wasn't contacted by Elaine."

"Who called? Her husband?"

Mom looked suddenly depleted to the point of emptiness. Silence descended.

"Mom?" Continued silence. "Mom?"

His mother stared from the kitchen window into a sunlit void. It was then that the boy spotted the open letter on the table beside his mother. He picked it up and took it to his room.

Dear Dorothy,

Your recent visit brought Elaine the only happiness she has known since the passing of our dear daughter last year. She was so very happy to see you and meet your lively son—but that momentary happiness was not sufficient to quell her grief. I'm very sorry to inform you that last week I came home from a business trip to discover Elaine had decided to join our little girl on the other side. They will not be returning to us.

Faithfully yours,

George

The boy returned to the kitchen and put his arm around his mother's shoulders, which were now shaking. "Don't cry, Mom. Please."

Her attempt at a response was stifled by deep, uncontrolled sobs.

"Everything's going to be OK. Mom? It's going to be OK. Really it is…"

The End

… of the innocence.

THE TROUBLE WITH CLIFF

The Sixties and All That

T he Air Canada 737 touched down lightly on the shimmering runway at the end of the six-hour flight from Toronto.
The screenwriter Teller, his wife and their infant son disembarked on a
ninety-day working visit that would stretch into an unimagined future.
Their first palm tree, first convertible, last cold winter; top down along
the Pacific Coast Highway; on to Topanga Canyon Boulevard; and three
winding miles more to Hillside Drive and their summer home. Their
landlord was a Topangan of long standing—an independent filmmaker

with a production company with no employees and three films in development. He preferred to work outside the "oppressive" studio system, he explained. What was not explained when they signed the lease was that he would be living next door in the attached guesthouse. No matter—he offered free advice on the mysteries of the Hollywood system, which seemed a great bonus. Meanwhile, there were more immediate concerns, like finding a daytime babysitter while Teller wrote and his wife attended post-natal exercise classes.

LOVING COUPLE WILL BABYSIT IN OUR CANYON SANCTUARY. REASONABLE RATES.

So read the classified ad in the *Topanga Messenger*. By great good fortune, it led to the bottom of their new street, the hand-carved sign TOPANGA RHAPSODY, and the home of Cliff and Marie—latter-day hippies keeping the faith these past twenty years. They were sturdy individualists, making them a perfect fit for Topanga Canyon, the motherland of LA counterculture. Joni Mitchell, Fleetwood Mac, assorted writers, composers and gurus called Topanga home. Thus the baby came to be left with Marie each afternoon while his father wrote, his mother exercised, and Cliff shared a little personal history with his new neighbor.

Cliff recounted his first meeting with Marie in the spring of '68 in the cafeteria of the Orion pictures building in Century City. Children of the sixties. It was her eyes that started the whole crazy thing. Cliff called them "Marie's headlights." They were oversized, widely spaced, and glowing day and night with an iridescent blue shimmering up from the ancient well of Marie's unbroken Scandinavian ancestry.

"Jesus—was I caught in the headlights!" said Cliff.

Romance will have its way. Soon they were an item: the reception-ist from Orion Pictures and the creative director from the Chiat/Day ad agency. Cliff had risen fast in the agency business—from copy as-sistant to full creative director in charge of the Mr. Clean account—in a scant four years. Marie was not impressed. She was a poet at heart, and corporate ladder-climbing held zero allure for her.

"Cliff, come on! You're better than Mr. Clean and you know it! You're meant for bigger things than filling a suit for Corporate America! My God, Cliff!" He loved it when she spoke his name.

She admired his intelligence, and he admired her poetry. Thanks to a photographic memory, Cliff was soon reciting her every poem. It was the highest compliment he could possibly pay.

SLEEP
> *Sleep, thou sweet salve of life*
> *Take me under thy silent spell*
> *And lead me through pleasant journeys of the night.*
> *Abandon me not to the cruelties of the conscious*
> *But lead me from the immediate*
> *To the sublime.*

Her antique Victorian verse sounded properly literary to his California ear: Cliff was smitten.

"That's beautiful, Baby. That's what it is. Beautiful!" he said.

Marie became Cliff's muse, his guide to a creative world where art trumped commerce each shining day. Marie had a plan: Goodbye, Orion Pictures; Goodbye, Chiat/Day. Farewell, studio apartment. Hello, City Hall wedding chapel. Hello, Topanga Canyon and the Beautiful People and the one-acre hillside plot for $9,250 with the stream running through it. All cash. No mortgage. No more 9 to 5. Freedom now, man! Marie had a plan...

Soon she was free to write, and Cliff was free to design and build their dream home. He was a proudly self-taught architect/builder with no time for the LA County Building and Safety: no building permits, no inspectors, no fuss. Another Topanga bonus: cool neighbors. Just up the hill was totally inexpensive medical care from the doctor who could handle everything but writing a prescription. Something about the medical board pulling his medical license for some lame reason. Living in Doc's guesthouse was Louise from Paris who made really cool jewelry, sold only to those she considered cool. Further up the road was Jerry the marriage counselor, an expert in his field thanks to his own four marriages. At the top of the hill, Farmer Phil, with his '52 Chevy truck and fifty orange trees that produced for everyone. Across Topanga Canyon Boulevard, the Barbarian Brothers: twin weightlifters discovered at Gold's Gym in Venice, now starring in low-budget martial arts movies. And down by Topanga Creek, Carpenter Carlos and his low-rent construction crew of illegal Guatemalans. A world unto itself: Topanga Canyon.

Soon after their arrival, a strange and charming thing began happening to Cliff: he was regularly mistaken for Neil Young. There had always been a resemblance blunted by the suit and tie Corporate America foisted on him. But now—hair longer, shoulders slouched, clad in blue jeans, flannel shirt and work boots—Cliff entered his full Neil Young phase. Fans approached him constantly:

"Just want to say I really love your work."

"Hey, Neil! *Harvest* changed my life, bro!"

"Cleveland? The concert for Tibet? I was there, man!"

At first he corrected them. "Oh, I'm not Neil. Sorry about that. Have a good day."

Bummer. Some smiled at their mistake, while others patted Cliff slyly on the arm or shoulder: "Mum's the word, man. No worries!"

They pressed a joint or two into his hand. Cliff brought it all back home to his muse. Marie enjoyed the masquerade.

"Why fight it, Cliff? If they thought you were Mr. Clean or the Pentagon God of War, that'd be a whole other matter! But Neil Young? Très cooool! Take a bow."

She bought him a Sharpie pen, and soon he was signing autographs. Rocking out without rocking. A twenty-something hippie chick approached him for an autograph at the local gas station. "Oh, go on, Neil. Make her day," said Marie.

The chick popped a perfect breast from her blouse, which Cliff promptly autographed. "How about the other one?" he asked playfully.

Marie yanked him away, yelling over her shoulder at the fan: "Who the Hell you think you are, bitch? Get a life!!"

For which Marie got the finger. Fame came with a price. Meanwhile, the poetry flowed freely.

TOPANGA RHAPSODY

> *Sweet, sweet Topanga*
> *Yawning gash of nature's bounty*
> *Soaring trunk of strength and life.*
> *Home to the high-flying hawk, the slithering snake,*
> > *the perennial poet,*
> *Take me unto thyself*
> *Transform my urban yearning into*
> *A tantric tsunami of peace and love.*
> *Take me Topanga…*
> *I am yours!*

Marie and her libido were flying. But as summer drifted into fall drifted into winter, Cliff grew distracted: less interested in the poetry, increasingly concerned with a dwindling cash flow…

"You can't remember my new poems? Pardon me? You used to recite every word I wrote!" The Muse was not amused.

"Maybe if you tried writing about construction costs? And add an upbeat ending while you're at it, OK?" said Cliff.

"Now he's a comedian! I'm going to forget you even said that, Clifford." When Marie was pissed, Cliff became 'Clifford.'

"Forgetting shouldn't be too hard with all the pot you've been smoking!" he said.

"You're—majorly regressing! I should dig out your corporate monkey suit and press it," she said.

"That's enough. Calm down, Marie."

His words had the opposite effect.

"Listen up, Mister—I didn't move from Corporate America to Topanga Canyon to spend my nights talking money! I'm a poet!"

"We're in a tight spot, Marie," said Cliff. "Sure, we live rent-free, no mortgage. But there are construction costs, property taxes, groceries, gas, my Merlot, your grass…"

"SHUT UP! I DON'T WANT TO HEAR ABOUT IT! WEREN'T YOU A CREATIVE DIRECTOR IN YOUR PAST LIFE? WEREN'T YOU?" Marie had strong lungs, energized by the oxygen-rich canyon air.

"Is your little history lesson going anywhere?" asked Cliff with a nervous grin.

"YOU BET IT IS! GET FUCKING CREATIVE, CLIFFORD!! GET THE MONEY THING TOGETHER! GO THERE!"

So Cliff got creative. Sunday found him five miles away at the Canoga Park Mall with a table and a stack of Neil Young albums—in full Neil regalia. Beside him was a large donation jar with a hand-drawn Peace Sign and the slogan Campaign For Nuclear Disarmament. Neil himself—in plaid and in person!

"That's right. I'm giving my music *away*, people. Just donate whatever you can to the cause. How would you like me to inscribe it?"

Cliff/Neil spread a tsunami of good vibes that day. Business was amazing. He was overwhelmed by his fellow Californians. The scruffier they were, the more they gave. Ninety minutes and thirty autographed albums later, Cliff was on his way back to Topanga with $628 in his Levis and a renewed faith in mankind.

Then reality came a-calling.

"Do you believe it, man? Mall cops! Like they don't have enough beggars and litterbugs to occupy their $7-an-hour time? Unbelievable! And what happened to freedom of expression?"

Cliff was booted out of the Canoga Park Mall.

"That's a shame. What did you do next?" asked his new neighbor .

"No problem! This was just the nudge I needed. The answer is bed spacers. I'm now into bed spacers, my friend!"

Blank stare from his audience of one. Cliff recounted a visit to the Philippines seven years earlier. "I'm in Buttfuck, Philippines, a hundred miles from Manila, hitching—it's dark. I bed down for the night by the roadway—wake up next morning in some old graveyard. Crypts like they have in New Orleans, above ground. Covered in vines. Kinda beautiful. I'm rolling up my sleeping bag, taking it all in when this young guy crawls out of a crypt not thirty feet away. Like the Second Coming of Christ. Stands up, yawns, stretches. I almost pissed my pants. He spots me—gives a little wave. I wave back. Next thing you know he's brewing up some tea beside his crypt."

"This is very weird. You making this stuff up, Cliff?" asked Teller.

"C'mon! How could I? Swear to God! Guy lives in the crypt. Been there three years. Along with a couple dozen crypt-kickin' neighbors! It's an abandoned graveyard—no visiting relatives. So these cats open up the old crypts, scrape out the human remains, sell whatever jewelry they find and move on in. On rainy nights, they pull the crypt covers closed to stay dry. Perfect. Just space enough for a single bed. That's why they're called bed spacers—get it? I'm introducing them to Topanga."

"You're selling timeshares in an old graveyard?"

"Ha, now that's funny! Why don't you ditch that screenplay you're working on and write about me?" Cliff had a healthy ego. "Lemme explain the plan. We get the occasional earthquake and wildfire here in So Cal, right?"

"I heard the rumor," said Teller.

"You Canadians born sarcastic? Or does playing second banana to Uncle Sam make you that way? Earthquakes—houses get leveled—people clear out fast, leaving behind perfectly sound fiberglass swimming pools. I've scooped a few pools up for free, moved them onto my land. Turning them into bed spacers for two—renting 'em out!"

A ton of bizarre information to absorb.

"Come on, I'll show you," said Cliff.

He led the way past his house with no walls to the rear of the spacious property, where Carpenter Carlos and his Guatemalan crew were digging a large hole to accommodate a fiberglass swimming pool.

"Swimming pools are curved like a VW Beetle, which gives them tremendous structural integrity. Pool's already got a drain in the bottom where we hook up the plumbing. Ease it into God's green earth, add a roof with skylights and an entry hatch like a submarine—voila! Swimming pool bed spacer. Like those crypts in the Philippines."

"You've actually done this. My God, it's genius, Cliff!" said Teller.

"I know. For the hippie masses: lining up all the way to the Pacific Coast Highway to kiss my low-rent ass."

Cliff was making money with his eccentric shelters. All very nice, but in her heart of hearts, Marie longed for the Cliff who remembered and recited her poetry, as he had during their courtship. She was a true romantic, and Cliff was losing sight of her essence amid all the construction and rental activity.

"You're charging too much rent, Cliff! They're just hippie kids! Come on—give them a break."

"First, not enough money, then we have too much? Give me a break, Marie," said Cliff.

"Listen to me. When we left Corporate America, it wasn't just a change of address. We left for a different lifestyle, for something truly meaningful," said his wife.

"Truly cool," said Cliff, as he went back to supervising his construction crew of illegal immigrants.

Marie went right on writing, becoming increasingly sardonic and contemporary. She was finding her voice, and in that voice, a sense of humor and proportion began to emerge. She began to gently and perceptively lampoon the foibles of her fellow Topangans. People were taking notice—including the *Topanga Messenger* weekly, which published her latest effort.

DAD'S BRAND-NEW DO
> *A great chunk of finance*
> *Tied to what is on top*
> *Salons, stylists,*
> *New looks that rock.*
> *Barbershops and brushes*
> *Ever so neat*

A brand-new do
For Dad to take to the street.
Stylish she was
And so well aware
Of the big first impression
Made by Cool Hair.
Their eyes locked
Her lips moistened
Into the space between them
Her words hastened:
"So sparse above
So perfect a dome
Time for a head shave
A new do to take home."
To Dad's great shock
And total dismay
Illusions of romance
Then and there slipped away.
As her golden tresses
To his now-angry eye
Turned to a Mohawk
And a full battle cry!

Cliff hated it. He had real difficulty keeping up with Marie's development as a writer. "You're making fun of my Neil Young 'do! Laughing at your husband for all the canyon to see!"

He waved the newspaper at her angrily. Marie was amazed. "Cliff—I am not making fun of anybody! It's just a little attempt at humor. To amuse people as they go about their day. Like e.e. cummings used to write. Calm down."

Cliff fixed a laser stare upon her. "Let me tell you something. Neil would never go to some beauty parlor or faggot-y hairdresser. He's got a cool, natural hippie look, and that's not gonna change, Marie, no matter what you think!"

"Please. It's not about you—or me. It's just a light piece of art, that's all."

He took a deep breath. "Art—well—that's different, isn't it? Here's something for you to hang in your art gallery."

Marie brightened. "What's that?"

Cliff held up the offending newspaper and tore it into quarter page pieces, which he gathered into a tidy pile. "If it's all right with you, I'm going to wipe my ass with these pieces of art. OK?"

In addition to his rental activities, Cliff took up Carpenter Carlos's suggestion of planting marijuana on his south-facing hillside.

"Big market for Mary Jane in the canyon, Señor Cliff," said Carlos.

Soon Cliff was truly in the money, thanks to a budding marijuana business. But sudden prosperity, as it often will, brought problems of its own.

"Free rent and a couple hundred a month don' do it for me no more, *amigo*." Carlos hungered for a larger slice of the American pie. "I need more *dinero*, Señor Cliff. I build houses for you, I farm Mary Jane for you. "

"And I pay you," said Cliff.

"Not enough, Señor. Two thousand a month would be better."

Carlos had dreams of his own that required more than Cliff was paying. Cliff took his measure. "You been smoking my shit, haven't you? Made you forget the day I found you in that tent down by the creek with the ass outta your trousers."

Carlos stood his ground. "Señor, I work hard for you."

"Yeah, it's called a job, Carlos. Welcome to America."

"And I take big risks for you. Any day somebody could call building inspector—or county sheriff to check out the little farm we got going."

Cliff did not welcome the veiled threats. "Now listen to me, Señor. I'll say this just once. You better make damn sure no authorities come a-calling on old Cliff. 'Cause if they do, the first phone call I'm making is to Immigration to hustle up here and deport your illegal ass back where it swam in from. *Comprendes?*"

Carlos looked at Cliff evenly, then flashed his best south of the border smile.

"Aw, Señor Cliff—Don' get loco—remember: we joined at the hip."

"What hip? What are you talking about?" asked his boss.

Carlos explained the underlying dynamic. "You know Mexican standoff? Two guys got guns on each other? Who's gonna pull the trigger? No winner, no loser. Mexican standoff. That's us, Señor Cliff! We joined at the hip."

Carpenter Carlos had a point.

The time came for the writer and his little family to move on. Cliff and Marie threw the going-away party. Everyone was there: the unlicensed doc, the filmmaker-landlord, Farmer Phil, Louise of French jewelry fame, Jerry the single marriage counselor, even the Barbarian Brothers, on hiatus between action films.

"We'll miss your poetry, Marie. You're really developing as a writer," said Teller's wife.

"That's so nice of you," said Marie.

"Why you leaving, man? You guys are total Canyon people," said Cliff.

"That's the trouble," said Teller. "Topanga torpor—somewhere between being relaxed and in a coma? Been losing track of time up here. I'm in the movie biz, Cliff. Have to move closer to Hollywood."

"Downsize; cut your overhead. Rent one of my bed spacers," suggested Cliff.

Next morning, the Canucks were gone.

—m—

As they will, twenty years flew by. Teller, firmly ensconced in LA, had remarried. Among assorted tales from the past, he had told his wife about Cliff and Marie and the early days in Topanga. Now: another New Year's Day. New year, old memories.

"Do you think they still live in Topanga?" asked his bride.

"Only way Cliff and Marie would ever leave that place is if they were dynamited out."

"How about paying them a visit?" she said.

Forty minutes and twenty miles later, they pulled up in front of the weathered TOPANGA RHAPSODY sign, next to a familiar and now sun-bleached '64 VW bug. On the back window a sign: SUPPORT OUR OOPS. The "TR" in troops had been removed.

"Now that's totally Cliff…" said the visitor.

On the bumper below: *Bush Sucks, Hillary Rocks*

They climbed the winding walkway to the house with no walls. To their left, the fire-charred hulk of a motor home lay in overgrown grass. They passed by in silence; she looked over at him uneasily. Cliff and Marie's TOPANGA RHAPSODY house, now vine-covered and sun-baked, loomed before them. A familiar whiskered face appeared over a railing.

"Here to see the rental?" Not a flicker of recognition.

"You showed me twenty years ago. Maybe you're asking too much."

Cliff paused, squinted, smiled. "Smartass Canadians. Where's Homeland Security when you need them?"

Teller presented Cliff with a bottle of Veuve Clicquot. "Happy New Year, brother."

"What took you so long?" said Cliff. He accepted the bottle without looking at it. His visitors stared in silent wonder at the house without walls, now packed with an impossible array of random objects, like the stuffed car of an LA homeless person on wheels. Cliff displayed no curiosity about his guest's new wife, the son Cliff and Marie used to babysit, or what the past twenty years had wrought. But he was a geyser of information about his favorite subject: himself.

"I'm here to tell you, Teller. This Neil Young thing has grown un-believably. It's like I've taken over Neil's public responsibilities. I mean,

Neil had stopped meeting his public years ago, so I do all that for him now. People love it, man. I get asked for autographs and get dinner invites by the dozen. Everybody digs my whole Neil thing big-time. Everybody except Marie, that is. I'm a star to everybody in Topanga—everybody except my ex-wife. Ha! And what's she up to? Her lame poetry, that's what. It's sad, man. She reads it to that dude Carlos who worked for me. Really pisses me off. What kind of artist prefers the opinion of a nobody to Neil Young?"

Silence like a rock. "Do you suppose you could show us the rental unit now?" asked Teller's wife.

Cliff led the way to a ramshackle trailer park of makeshift structures. He showed them to a rusty shipping container with a rough plywood interior, minimal light, four bunk beds, and a dusty kitchenette.

"Does it have a bathroom?" she asked.

"Down the path—shared with a few others. Looking for a rustic rental? Rest of the canyon's been bought up by yuppies. Very sad. Big ugly houses. If you want to see how crazy somebody is, let them build the home of their dreams. Very revealing." Cliff's spiel was interrupted by a drug-thin young couple.

"Hey, Cliff." They nodded tentatively at the visitors.

"You got it?" asked Cliff.

"All cash," said the skinny tenant through methamphetamine teeth. His companion was a pretty girl just out of her teens, wearing pajama bottoms, sipping a Corona. The tenant handed over a roll of cash; Cliff silently counted.

"How you doin'?" asked the young woman of nobody in particular.

The visitors drove off in somber silence.

"Cliff smelled," said Teller's wife.

They turned in at a large house up the hill from TOPANGA RHAPSODY, where an attractive middle-aged lady was clipping red rose bushes. Louise the French jewelry-maker greeted her former neighbor warmly. Soon, they were in her studio sipping wine and reminiscing. Louise had stayed in touch with Marie.

"Oh, yes, she's one of my best customers. She and Carlos have a lovely home in the country outside San Diego. Carlos built their Spanish dream home and to this day loves listening to her poetry."

"Cliff says Carlos was the only one dumb enough to listen to Marie's 'lame' poetry," said Teller.

"The split was nasty: Cliff was arrested and held in jail for three days. He came after Carlos with a gun the same day he found her and Carlos inside the motor home. She was just reciting her poetry to him. Cliff went wild, said she was coming on to Carlos with her dirty love poems. She's still very wary of Cliff; lets on she's homeless. You must never tell Cliff where they live."

"Wow."

She topped up their wine glasses.

"Louise—ever wonder about the trouble with Cliff? Like, what's really going on there...?"

"Marie used to ask me that. She felt responsible—said Cliff was always edgy—angry. Always about little things. She wondered what she was doing wrong, what she should be doing differently. Was she putting too much economic pressure on him? Being unsupportive of his Neil Young thing? I told her, 'Honey, you're asking the wrong questions. Stop blaming yourself. The trouble with Cliff isn't you.'"

"What do you suppose it is?" asked Teller's wife.

The longtime neighbor smiled.

"Quite simple, actually. **The trouble with Cliff—is Cliff.**"

The End

... of a hippie dream, Man.

MAROONED IN MALIBU

Fabled Sands Yield A Showbiz Secret

The Hollywood announcement was big news in old Montréal: **LOCAL FILM NOMINATED FOR ACADEMY AWARD!** The tale of a doomed love affair between a beautiful young woman and a tormented Catholic priest, *Shades of Love* was controversial, fearless and stylish, which earned it a Best Foreign Film nomination. And made its thirty-something writer-director Peter Anderson and his wife, Paulette Bourgeois, the film's star, instant celebrities. Next morning, the newshounds were at their doorstep.

THE GAZETTE: How does it feel to wake up an Academy Award nominee?

THE DIRECTOR: Pleasantly shocking! It does grab one's attention. But let me say right off the top, full credit goes to my beautiful wife, Paulette, for the performance of the decade, and to the Canadian film funding agencies for making our movie possible.

THE GAZETTE: Are you ready for Hollywood?

THE DIRECTOR: It's like being told to pack for a voyage to the moon, frankly! We've never been to Tinseltown—isn't that shocking? Never been there. Too busy right here putting together our home-grown movies. Now all of a sudden we're astronauts hurtling straight for Planet Hollywood!

THE STAR: With Peter at the controls we'll be just fine...

Three weeks later, they boarded Air Canada Flight 650 non-stop to Los Angeles. Anderson was a white-knuckle flyer.

"Did you pack my meds, Paulette? Did you!? I must maintain my director's cool!"

The rising star at his side checked her eyeliner in a heart-shaped compact. "I feel like I'm heading home, not leaving it," she said in her charming Québec accent.

Her enormous brown eyes brimmed with anticipation. He had discovered her in his doctor's outer office shortly after she left the village of her birth to become a big city receptionist. Later he would joke that a colonoscopy brought them together. Today he glanced over at her nervously.

"You're so very beautiful, my dear," he said.

She snapped her compact shut. "This light is terrible," she said. The last word sounded especially charming in her French accent.

Their suite at the Beverly Wilshire overflowed with bouquets from instant friends: talent agents, managers, publicists, casting directors—show business hustlers of every persuasion. The Hollywood Welcome Wagon. Cellophane-wrapped fruit baskets sufficient to feed a Third World classroom glistened in the luminous southern California light. She crossed to the huge window and peered down at the Mercedes and BMW's floating by.

"Wilshire Boulevard. Rodeo Drive—right down there..." she said dreamily.

"Where are my meds? Could I have your attention for a moment?" said Anderson, scrabbling amid the toiletries for a Valium.

That night at the nominees' reception, they met stars, directors and producers by the dozen—all greeting them warmly as equals.

"Everyone is so nice! *Merveilleux!* So very friendly!" she enthused.

"*En garde*, Paulette. There are sharks among the mermaids. And piranhas aplenty," said her director darkly.

"Where?" she said with real concern.

"Don't worry. Just stick with me." And she did.

Next day at the show's rehearsal, they were elated to be seated next to a major film star and immediately behind Julia Roberts. The star addressed them easily.

"How are ya? What brings you kids here?"

"Best Foreign Film nomination," said Peter.

"Good job! I love directors from outside the USA. Doing a picture with Antonioni in Italy right now... know him?"

"I do not," said Peter.

"Neither do I," said the star, laughing. "Angelo's a little strange. But that's what I love about the guy!"

Anderson laughed stiffly.

"And what, may I ask, is your name?" said the star, leaning in towards Anderson's beautiful wife.

Their decidedly dark film lost to the Swedish entry, a coming-of-age story set in a small town populated by inoffensive dreamers. After the ceremony, they were thrown directly into the serious business of film industry socializing.

"How did you like our picture?" Paulette asked a bearded producer.

"You must remember Hollywood is the home of the happy ending, my dear. Your character dousing herself in kerosene and going up in flames over her priest lover-boy was a bit tough to take," said the producer. "But you were beautiful, Baby! Barbecued or not! Here, take my card."

That night back in the Beverly Wilshire, Peter and Paulette enjoyed the best sex of their lives. Next morning at breakfast, along with the French toast and formally dressed waiters, was the hometown reporter.

THE GAZETTE: So what's up next for Peter and Paulette?

THE DIRECTOR: Back to Montréal to continue work on my next movie.

THE GAZETTE: We're not losing you to Hollywood?

THE DIRECTOR: Never! Although I do have a Hollywood agent now...

THE GAZETTE: And Paulette?

THE STAR: I'm really not sure. I met some interesting people. We'll see…

They were signed by the fabled William Morris Agency, in the person of the well-connected Arnie the Agent. He invariably made in excess of 80 phone calls a day and two major deals a week. Paulette was first to receive a firm Hollywood offer: cast in a lead role by MGM with a second picture in negotiation with Paramount. Within three weeks, the Academy Award-nominated couple had repacked their bags and departed Montréal for good.

As an Academy Award nominee, Anderson was up for several directing assignments, but deals were slow to materialize. He considered himself an "auteur" director and began to insist on pitching his own projects. Arnie the Agent demurred.

"I'm telling you, Peter. Every star, writer and director's got a pet project in this town. And guess what? The studios don't really give a shit. Hitch yourself to a studio project that's already got a green light. That's how careers are built here."

"Remember my last movie?" said Anderson. "There was a pet project that didn't do so badly."

The agent flicked a piece of imaginary lint from his Armani suit.

"Get real. *Shades of Love* is an art film. Won't make any money. We make pictures for the whole freakin' planet here—not just friends and family. Think global like the studios, my friend. And global isn't some edgy little Canadian flick where some depressive chick sets herself on fire over the horny hometown priest who won't elope with her."

Anderson peered at his high-energy agent bemusedly. "You're colorful, Arnie. I'll give you that. Very colorful," said the director.

"Well, thanks a bunch," said the man from William Morris.

The agent gave his client an appraising look. "Where did you go to school, Peter? Me, I'm a graduate of HKU: Hard Knocks University. How about yourself?"

"Oxford, actually—over in England?"

"I know where it is," said the agent matter-of-factly.

"I attended on a Rhodes Scholarship."

"That's nice. Can all that get you a film deal? Why do you need me?" replied the man in Armani.

—⚭—

Peter and Paulette spent that evening at the Polo Lounge in Beverly Hills.

"Arnie got me an audition on a new Aaron Spelling TV series. It's very exciting!" said Paulette.

"No, it's not," said Peter. "We're movie people. Be careful with that TV work. Next thing you know, he'll have you in a nun's habit flying across the Australian outback. Or on a broomstick to sort out people's love lives! You're destined for better than that, Paulette. Don't let the Hollywood hacks hack you to pieces."

The actress's beautiful brown eyes fluttered nervously. "Did Arnie have anything for you?"

"Let me put it this way. I'm currently helping poor Arnie set his sights a little higher, my darling. And you should, too."

—⁓—

Twenty years passed. A deeply tanned, perfectly-manicured hand picked up the phone in the posh Malibu Colony beach house.

"Nick from the Gazette? No!! How wonderful to hear from you after all these years! You're coming to town when? Lucky us! I'll have my assistant bring you out to Malibu for cocktails and a good gossip!"

About to retire from journalism, the frumpy film critic had secured a final plum assignment from *The Gazette*.

A gleaming gray Jaguar glided to the end of Sunset Boulevard, turned right at Gladstone's Restaurant, then headed up the Pacific Coast Highway. The reporter looked at the director's assistant behind the wheel, her blonde hair framed by the rolling surf in the background.

"Peter never stops. He writes all morning, attends to business and meetings in the afternoon—he never stops so, of course, I never stop!"

"Is he directing?" said the reporter.

"Not at the moment. Mainly writing, developing, meeting with producers and financiers. Big, big projects. His current one is an archaeological thriller—*Indiana Jones* meets *The Bourne Identity*. He has some major talent attached and two studios fighting over it."

"My, my," said the reporter.

"But it's all very hush-hush."

With a nod from the guard, the Jaguar rolled through the Malibu Colony security gate. They turned to the right and headed along a quiet beachside lane.

"That's Sting's place, that's Matthew McConaughey, Pamela

Anderson is over there, Streisand is the pink one up ahead, there's Larry Hagman's from Dallas, that's the director—James Cameron—and here we are—home at last!"

"Will I see Paulette today?" said the reporter.

"On location," said the assistant.

They pulled in at a homey two-storey Cape Cod with two parking spots—one hosting a steel gray Mini Cooper convertible and the other, the Jag. They reached a blue door that opened as if on cue. A white-haired, deeply tanned older version of Peter Anderson greeted them.

"Nick Elson, reporter extraordinaire! You simply have not aged a day! How ARE you?"

They shook hands and Anderson ushered Nick through a casually beautiful living room, a dining room with polished tree trunk chairs around a gleaming crystal table, and onward to an outdoor deck. Surf thumped, sailboats sailed, dolphins danced, a sitcom star waved from the deck next door, and Peter Anderson beamed. "What's missing from this picture?" he said.

"Nothing whatsoever?" exclaimed the guest.

"Strawberry margaritas!" said Anderson.

The assistant scurried off on her mission as Anderson and his guest sank into impossibly comfortable deck chairs.

"We never see you in Montréal, Peter. Now I understand why," said the reporter.

The director laughed in the practiced way of department store Santas. "Well—yes—this is all very nice, of course. But the reality of life in Malibu is the work—the screenplays, the story meetings with producers and studios, meetings with lawyers and accountants, reporters like yourself, the foreign video deals and dubbing of my Canadian films—do you know they love my stuff in Korea and Japan? It's endless! Fortunately, there's the beach for those precious moments away from the rat race."

The assistant returned with margaritas in glasses the size of cereal bowls.

"Thank you, nurse!" said the ever-chipper director.

The reporter raised a chilled glass and a hot topic. "When will we see you and Paulette working together again?"

The director peered in the general direction of Hawaii.

"Well—dear Paulette—she's been doing television for some time now—TV movie thingies—you know. It's another world, really. I'm feature films—no television. Sorry."

A sunny silence descended.

"Would it be fair to say your career has evolved from directing to writing and developing?" said the reporter.

"Absolutely. I write every day without fail. Screenplays, treatments, rewrites, adaptations..."

"I hear the studios treat you screenwriters well," said the reporter.

Anderson chuckled. "Let's just say the rent and groceries are covered," he said.

"But don't the studios interfere with the creative process? You know, creation by committee and all that?" said the reporter.

"Not if you know how to manage them, Nick. How to handle them.

I tell them I'd love to hear their little ideas—just write them on the back of the check," said Anderson cheerfully.

The reporter laughed. "Consider yourself quoted. By the way, is there a credit list I could see?" he asked.

"I'm sorry, but most of what I do is very hush-hush, Nick. The studios are highly competitive and secretive about their development slates. But leave your card with my assistant; she'll be in touch."

"Thank you. Are you still with William Morris?" said the reporter.

"Lord, no!" said Anderson. "My man there started doing television! After that I simply gave up on the poor fellow. Paulette still uses him, but not me. No, I use the best entertainment attorney in the business. All the A-list people use attorneys. It's the only way to maintain control of your career," said Anderson.

—⚍—

The next morning the reporter awoke in his hotel room with a reporter's instinct; he made a call. An hour later he was at William Morris on El Camino Drive, talking with Arnie the Agent.

"Paulette goes from project to project. She's always working. Still beautiful, and directors love her," said Arnie.

"Wonderful," said the reporter. "And Peter has developed quite a career for himself in the twenty years since his nomination—writing, directing, the beach house in Malibu. Are you sorry he left the agency?"

The agent's eyes widened. "Hello!? You smoking some of that weird Canadian shit? What freakin' career? The guy hasn't worked in twenty years! Only wanted to direct his own stuff. I arranged dozens of meet-ings—his ideas are uncommercial. Gimme a break!" said the agent.

The reporter was visibly jarred. "But what about all his screenplay deals?"

"What deals? I tried to sell him as a writer too. Zilch! He's never sold a single screenplay or pitch! Nada! Zero! Big goose egg!"

The reporter was reeling. "But—the production company—the personal assistant—the beach house in Malibu..."

"Smoke and mirrors, Baby! Hollyweird BS!" said Arnie. "All thanks to Paulette's acting gigs! Cash talks, and bullshit walks. Marrying her is the only—repeat *only*—successful move that guy made in the last 20 years! She bought the house in Malibu with deals I made for her, not him. And he still craps on me to this day, does he not? Says I couldn't get him work. But whose fault was that? We're not miracle workers here at Morris. We don't hire the talent—the studios do that."

The reporter sat in shocked silence as the agent continued. "Look, I don't mean to be too hard on somebody who's spent the last 20 years knocking on closed doors. But the guy has moved into total fantasy world territory, you know? A legend in his own mind. All the trappings of success—thanks to his wife—except for the track record or talent. Hello!?"

The next morning dawned bright and beautiful. LA—home to the upwardly mobile and downwardly spiraling—was once again on the move. A black Lincoln Town Car rolled down Sunset Boulevard en route to Paramount for a 7 a.m. makeup call. Inside, Paulette Bourgeois reviewed her lines for the day's shoot.

At the Sports Club LA, Arnie the Agent negotiated by phone with a producer in New York while doing his early morning treadmill.

"No—five points on the back end, Harry—five points and you got a deal with Paulette. Anything less, you get chopped liver. "

High above it all, a silver and red Air Canada DC 10 lifted away from the City of Angels. Cocooned inside, a reporter organized his notes for the feature story:

PAULETTE BOURGEOIS: 20-YEAR STAR SHINES BRIGHTLY.

Far beneath the spreading vapor trail, a lean, tanned older gentleman completed his morning jog across the fabled sands of Malibu. Soon he would ascend to his luxurious home office overlooking the eternal Pacific to put the final touches on his seventeenth unsold screenplay.

Ever the hometown star—flickering faintly from afar—living the Tinseltown dream.

The End

... of a Hollywood phony.

LARRY'S LAST RIDE
From the Mountains to the Sea

Those first three years in LA saw the spec screenplays fly from Teller's word processor one by one in search of a Hollywood home, while his life savings evaporated in the warm California sun. For the first time since he left for college, he called his faraway father for help. The retired Mountie graciously obliged; the screenwriter remained at his keyboard for one last movie proposal. As Teller wrote, he gazed out at the young wife and blond-haired baby boy playing on the evergreen lawn. The joy of the work now crowded by a sense of urgency. Then it happened.

"It's a good story. I like it. This we can put into development."

Teller peered across a prairie of beige carpeting to The Man behind the big desk. He was the son and namesake of a famous western movie star from the forties and fifties. And currently the very low-key and anodyne president of a major Hollywood movie studio. It was a done deal. The writer's agent and producer beamed. Handshakes all round. As the pitch meeting broke up, The Man turned to the writer.

"Did they validate your parking?

"That won't be necessary, sir. I've just been validated."

Smiles and chuckles. A six-figure writing contract in hand. Not such a bad day.

—⁂—

Three months later: screenplay finished; money in the bank; time for that first slice of the American pie. LA real estate was out of reach. But eighty miles along the Pomona Freeway was the turnoff to a mountain community offering blue skies, green pines and down-to-earth prices. The Ponderosa pines were taller and the skies bluer, but this place was closer to his small-town northern background than LA could ever be; Teller felt at home.

A sixties mountain cabin with a wood-shingled roof, massive stone fireplace and a spectacular starlit deck called out to him. Teller purchased it from a kindly older couple who had evicted their biker son named Pony for non-payment of his $200 rent. Pony was famous on the mountain for lateness: late rent, late for work, late-night parties, lateness at court. The clock was clearly not Pony's friend. Though he never appeared at the cabin after the sale, Pony's mojo lingered on in the form of beer cans in odd places, sheets nailed over windows, a shoe or two decorating the shingled roof, and a lovesick former girlfriend turning up at odd hours in avid pursuit of Pony and his secret charms.

The neighbors greeted Teller and his family with a mixture of mountain hospitality and massive relief: handshakes, pies, cookies, barbecue and fishing invitations. At the head of the Welcome Wagon were Pam, the pretty blonde RE/MAX agent who had sold them the property, and her hillbilly husband, Larry. Pam came from a good family in San Diego and had met Larry twelve years earlier when she was a recent college grad living the single life in Redondo Beach. Four young guys occupied the apartment next to Pam and her roommates. The most attentive was the wiry, courtly one from Arkansas with the red hair and easy Southern drawl.

"Name's Larry. I'm just an Arkansas hillbilly got bitten by a big ole surfin' bug!"

She found him utterly charming. Larry wasted no time concluding Pam's law school boyfriend was "just not treatin' her rat (right)." Larry then told the boyfriend if he didn't "start treatin' that girl rat" he'd whisk Pam away to a better place. That evenly delivered ultimatum led to a bloody fistfight on the Redondo Beach Boardwalk, which the boyfriend decisively lost. Everyone present—not just the defeated one—noted Larry's cool demeanor and fast fists.

They married and moved a hundred miles from the beach to a small town 5,000 feet up in the San Gabriel Mountains in Riverside County. Soon enough they were a family of four. But in addition to his bride, Larry carried a major secret with him up that mountain. First, his name was not Larry at all. He never disclosed his birth name to her, and she accepted that. Second, he was an escapee from the Louisiana State Penitentiary where he was one year into an eleven-year sentence for grand theft auto. Larry and several associates stole ninety cars in seventy-two hours from the streets of Shreveport and dropped them at a secret location for wholesale shipment to Russia. But somebody talked. So Larry and his pals ended up in Louisiana State—the meanest maximum security prison in the good ole USA—where Larry got to sharpen his fighting skills. But how did he manage to leave the Alcatraz of the South ten years early?

"Just like you would; I walked out. Guard swung the main gate open and wished me luck."

"Nice guard," said the writer.

"Lordy, no! None of them in there was nice. It's not called the Alcatraz of the South for nothing! But fifteen large will mellow a guard out for a day."

Larry set himself up after his "release" as the Mountain Locksmith. "Me—a locksmith! Now ain't that a hoot? Money's not good as my car business was, but there's a lot less down time!"

Hillbilly humor delivered with an ever-easy Southern drawl. They sipped their Coors on Teller's deck, under the starry blanket overhead.

"Larry, we've become good friends."

"That's the truth, Hollywood." Larry favored nicknames.

"And I really appreciate you taking me into your confidence. But—that's one helluva secret you're carrying."

Larry smiled. "FBI would agree with you. I've pulled off what Butch and Sundance tried to do, you know? Disappear! Into thin mountain air. Now if those boys had lived a little longer, don't you figure they woulda loved that movie? They'd be takin' a big bow! Doin' show-and-tell at their kids' school! Meet and greet at shopping centers! TV commercials for Citibank!"

Teller smiled.

"Listen up, Hollywood. You're the writer. I'm talking sequel here: BUTCH AND SUNDANCE: THE SUNSET YEARS."

Larry had Hollywood's attention.

"Only problem is them boys got themselves killed! Where's the Hollywood ending? So what we need's a brand-new true-life story along the same lines but with a whole different ending—hear me out now, here she comes: CAR THIEF TO HAPPY PAPPY: LARRY RIDES AGAIN."

The writer burst out laughing. Larry looked on appraisingly.

"Is that a 'You're one stupid hillbilly' laugh? Or a 'Why didn't I think of that myself' kinda laugh?"

"OK. I've seen pitches a whole lot weaker get into development—and production," said Hollywood.

"You're not just pullin' poor ole Larry's leg?"

Teller shook his head. The improbable duo fell silent.

"So when we goin' to work, Hollywood?"

Next morning, Teller manned his laptop while Larry paced the floor. He talked four days non-stop. A massive dam constructed twelve years earlier suddenly burst, releasing a flood of vivid memory. Larry barely paused for food.

"Come on, man, time for lunch," said the writer.

"Don't feel like eatin' lately. Hey, can we do a video of when Pam and me met? Good girl from good family meets bad boy from nowhere? Be a nice keepsake for my kids."

They taped ninety minutes of courtship and marriage anecdotes, great stuff: GOODY TWO-SHOES FALLS FOR THE FUGITIVE.

Next morning Teller appeared at Larry's door. Larry received him propped up in a big brass bed watching TV.

"Hollywood! Welcome to Hillbilly Heaven."

"Getting lazy in your old age? It's past ten," said the writer.

"All that talkin' tuckered me out. What's up?"

"The mouse has roared. Gotta head back to LA for awhile."

"Translate that for a simple hillbilly, will you?"

"My agent got me a writing assignment at Disney. Need to be there for meetings and story conferences. Take about six weeks."

Larry lifted his red head and sniffed the air. "I smell something—kinda strong—fresh and pleasant…"

Hollywood took a whiff. "What?"

Larry flashed that Southern smile. "Cash! Greenbacks! Filthy lucre! Congratulations."

"Thank you."

"Say hi to Mickey for me. But don't stay off this ole mountain too long now, hear? We got work to do. Got us a movie to write!"

The screenwriter did Disney's bidding: Mickey's checks cleared the bank; Teller headed back up the mountain to his favorite fugitive. As before, Pam opened the front door. But this time, she stepped outside for a private word.

"He's been looking forward so much to seeing you. Can't stop talking about it. But you're going to notice a change in Larry. I just want you to take a deep breath—try not to look surprised."

"What's the matter?"

"He'll tell you himself. Doesn't like me talking about it; we better hustle back in."

As before, Larry was propped up in bed watching TV. "Give my regards to Mickey?"

"You know I did," said Hollywood. But he couldn't disguise his shock at his friend's sunken face and emaciated torso.

"Didn't your Mammy tell you it ain't polite to stare?"

"What's going on, old buddy?"

"Too much Southern fried according to the Doc. Not enough

broccoli. Bad for my colon. But that's just his opinion. Sawbones gotta render a fancy opinion with his fancy bill now, don't he?"

Even cancer received the light Southern treatment.

"I'm sorry."

"Hey, Hollywood, pull your kisser up off the floor! There's a sunny side to all this—lookee here!" Larry opened his pajama top below his left shoulder revealing a plastic box the size of a cigarette pack. It was connected to a clear tube that disappeared directly into his chest.

"My new toy! Morphine pump. Here comes the sun—24/7! Party time at Larry's!"

His friend stood speechless. Larry continued. "Enough chitchat. Ready to get back to work?"

Pam entered the bedroom bearing a tray with juice and tea.

"Thank you, darlin'. Ain't she grand? If I make it to Heaven one fine day—and that's no slam dunk—I'm gonna walk through them Pearly Gates right on into this here angel's arms. And if she's not right there waiting and all I get's Saint Peter or one of those other long-faced dudes—then I'm demanding a full refund on my ticket! Yes I am!"

They laughed. Hollywood turned to Pam.

"Where did he learn to spin yarns like that?"

Larry jumped in. "When I was a youngster down in Arkansas! No TV, no movies, no newspaper. Just the radio and each other. We talked, played music, told stories..."

"And he's never stopped!" said his wife.

"Hey, I got a special request," said Larry.

"Let's hear it," the writer said.

"You know I love the good ole USA. Always have, always will. But gotta admit I'm a little embarrassed I never been outside the lower 48. It's a big ole world. Like to lay eyes on a little more of it. Only I can't be gettin' a passport. Slight problem with Uncle Sam. But you don't need a passport to cross that border to old Mexico. Just a travelin' buddy. What say?"

Traveling with Larry? A huge medical issue...

"Can I think about this overnight?" said Hollywood.

Larry ploughed on. "There's a place called Rosarito Beach right south of Tijuana. Four-hour drive. We can write full tilt every day on the beach. Fancy that! Writin' a Hollywood movie on the sands of old Mexico! My friend Skinny Kenny'll come with us to take care of my meds and the food. Kenny's a good ole boy. My very own personal assistant. Free us up to write and party."

Outside on the doorstep Pam spoke. "It's entirely up to you. Either way he'll understand."

"How much time does he have?"

"The doctor said a month, maybe a bit more."

"Does Larry know this?"

His wife nodded. "Doc's in his office right now if you'd care to speak with him."

Hollywood faced the sixty-something small-town doctor in his modest office.

"I've never seen a cancer move quite this quickly. He'll be no better or worse on a road trip, except it'd be good for his spirits. Will he survive the trip? There are no guarantees here. I've dealt with a case or two of Americans passing away in Mexico. Total nightmare. Family had to pay bribes to get the body sent back promptly. If Larry doesn't make it, you need to be prepared to load him into the back seat and drive him across the border at night like he's asleep. Have his ID and several hundred in cash in hand. That's it."

Next morning, Larry was on his feet, his bathrobe obscuring the emaciation.

"Old Sawbones lay on the gloom and doom? Hah! Shoulda been an end-of-the-world preacher. So what's the verdict, Hollywood?"

"Don't mean to make a bad joke—but there's only one reason for actually doing this crazy thing."

"What's that?" asked Larry.

"You're just dying to go to old Mexico."

Black humor on a sunny California day. Awkward pause, followed by a burst of uncontrolled laughter that made everything OK. Twenty-four hours later, and they were freewheeling down the mountain en route to the San Diego Freeway and the Mexican border. The top on the second-hand convertible was down as it barreled along; a banshee sound rose from the passenger seat.

"YEEEEE YIP! YIP! YEEEE HAAAA!"

Larry was in fine form.

"That there's a rebel yell!" piped up Skinny Kenny.

"Must be great for getting the attention of waiters," shouted Hollywood over the wind.

"How do you writer guys come up with your ideas? I always wondered about that," said Kenny, a disheveled, distracted version of Larry.

"I generally find them where I'm not looking," said the writer.

"Leave the man alone! Pass me up another beer, boy!" said the patient.

Kenny obliged.

"What line of work you in, Kenny?" asked the ever-curious Teller.

"Peace of mind. Asset protection. Ultimate home security..." Larry jumped in.

"Skinny's a termite's worst nightmare. Schwarzenegger may be the Terminator. But this guy's the EXterminator! One notch above Arnold, right, Skinny?"

"Make fun all you want, Larry. I provide an essential service," Skinny Kenny intoned solemnly.

"YIP YIP YEEEEEEE HAAAAAAW!!" replied Larry.

Two hours later found them thirty miles south of the border, and a world apart. Larry and Hollywood faced off over two giant margaritas on the outdoor patio of their oceanfront hotel. Sunshine danced with impossible brilliance on the rolling waters below.

"Mexico! We did it!"

Larry was tickled.

"Where'd Kenny disappear to?" asked Teller.

"Pharmacy shopping. They don't bother with prescriptions down here, and Skinny's old lady loves those pain pills. Help her chill out. If you was married to that battle-ax, believe me, you'd wanna help her chill out, too! Ole Kenny's a saint, God bless him." Hollywood laughed. "One helluva musician too. Skinny plays a fine fiddle. But he got the worst case of stage fright. Damn shame. Keeps him from playing in public. That boy could go straight to the Opry."

Larry took a sip from his margarita.

Teller responded, "Not just Kenny. There are people all across the country who have the talent to take a run at Hollywood—become writers, directors, actors—but never will."

"How come?" asked Larry.

"Stage fright. Never been noticed or encouraged. Too busy supporting a family. Afraid to leave home and head west…"

Larry harbored no such fears. "First thing tomorrow, we're right back at work. Morning's my best time," he said.

Hollywood looked him squarely in the eye.

"How are you feeling, buddy?"

He tapped the morphine pack under his shirt pocket.

"Frisky as a billy goat with two dicks."

A waiter materialized at Larry's shoulder.

"Pardon, Señors…"

"Don't sneak up on me like that, Pancho. I could be packing heat," said Larry.

The waiter flashed a gold-toothed grin.

"Señoritas invite you for tequila."

Two attractive sisters three tables over sending smiles their way…

The foursome shared a fine dinner. Larry, basking in a Hollywood-Mexican glow, explained proudly they were here to work on a movie project.

Their beachfront morning story session found Larry in top form.

"Hey, man, cool thing about this morphine pack—it totally kills hangovers!"

"Lucky guy," replied the suffering scribe.

"Wanna trade places?" said Larry.

Larry was tickled with their work environment.

"Fancy this—pounding out a fine old yarn on a beach in ole Mexico! Who we writing this for—Disney? MGM? Paramount? And how we gonna know when we're done?"

Hollywood looked up from his laptop.

"We're done here when we get to the end of this outline. Another four, five days. Then ten more days back home on the first draft. Then my agent takes charge and shops it all over town to the highest bidder."

"All right! Now check this out wanna hear how I boosted my first ride?" said the retired grand theft auto expert.

"You bet. But first—how you really feeling?"

"Look—people get over the Big C all the time, man. You see me fussin' and frettin'? Your writing partner's got a very high-powered medical team workin' overtime! Don't you be worryin'! This posse's charging fast forward to fame and fortune. Hear me?!"

Hollywood had to smile. Later that night, Skinny Kenny and

Hollywood were bearing takeout food from the hotel restaurant back to the room Kenny and Larry shared.

"He says he's not hungry, but put it in front of him, he'll eat," said Kenny.

"He had a big day. Working, driving, shopping, dancing—never stopped," said the writer.

"That's Larry," said Kenny.

"How did you guys meet?"

"Old lady got mad at me one time and took off for her mother's. Changed the locks on me before she left. Had to call the locksmith. Larry got me back in in under two minutes. Been friends ever since."

Kenny unlocked the door; they entered the darkened bedroom.

"Hey, Lar—chow time!" said Kenny.

No response. Larry lay motionless under a sheet drawn to his chin.

"C'mon, buddy; get it while it's hot!" said Teller.

No response. Kenny drew close and bent down. Not a breath of a breath.

"Oh, Jesus—no—no."

"I know CPR," said Hollywood. "Step aside!" He pulled the sheet down to waist level. "The morphine pack's over his heart…"

"Pull it off! Do it!" yelled Kenny.

Larry's eyes popped open. "Don't you dare!" he said.

"You crazy sonofabitch!" said the writer.

"Guilty! Guilty, Your Honor!" said Larry through his laughter.

Next morning found them again at work on the beach. Larry, in sunglasses, sombrero, bathing suit and crisp new sport shirt paced the warm sands and reminisced while the writer typed intently.

"How we doing, Hollywood?"

"Great. Two more days and we're there."

Two waiters approached from the direction of the hotel bearing loaded trays. Behind them came Skinny Kenny.

"Right on time," Teller said.

Larry's friend had arranged a surprise catered lunch. "Love your office, guys," said Kenny.

"Check it out," said Hollywood, pointing beyond the surf.

A pod of dolphins broke the surface. Suddenly for a magic instant, one leapt free of the shimmering Pacific glistening in the sunshine.

"Show-off in every crowd," said Larry.

One waiter cleared away the dishes, while the other topped up the champagne. Skinny Kenny got to his feet.

"I'd like to propose a toast on this beautiful day. To my good friend Larry, who makes sure I'm never locked outta my own life."

Glasses were raised. "To Larry!"

Larry rose. "And I'd like to propose a toast: to the Good Lord who makes sure I'm never locked inside anyplace I'd rather not be! Thank you, Lord!"

Kenny bent down, opened the small case at his feet and extracted a gleaming red fiddle.

"Go for it, Skinny!" exclaimed Larry.

The musician raised the fiddle to his shoulder, flexed his fingers and began to play. An old Irish air flowed forth effortlessly and beautifully: *Danny Boy*. Kenny created harmonics that matched the sound of two fiddles playing together: an extraordinary, entrancing performance. Then he smoothly shifted to Jerry Lee Lewis: *Whole Lotta Shakin' Goin' On*. Just as fine. A Mexican memory for a lifetime.

Next morning, Larry and Hollywood took breakfast on the patio.

"Where's Skinny?" said Hollywood.

"Got into Señor Tequila big time last night," said Larry. "Look for him round about noon."

"Mexico will do that to you," said Hollywood.

Larry's gaze shifted from the patio to the shoreline.

"Big ole world, ain't it? I gotta thank you, Hollywood, for getting' me outta my man cave up there on that mountain. Gonna beat this thing. I'm gettin' better every passing day—I feel it. Gonna bring the wife and kids down here. They'd love Mexico…"

They finished their final story session at their beachfront office. Teller snapped his laptop shut.

"Sure you got enough?" said Larry.

"Absolutely no problem. Gotta do that first draft now. Give me ten days."

Hollywood was packing his suitcase when Larry burst into his hotel room.

"Lordy, we got ourselves a problem!"

A moment later, they were in the room next door where two days earlier Larry had played dead. They looked down at Skinny Kenny in the adjoining bed. A depleted jug of tequila with a rattlesnake coiled in the bottom was on the bedside table, flanked by a vial of pills. Several red pills were scattered about randomly. Teller reached down and put his hand on Kenny's calm cold forehead.

"How?" said the incredulous Teller.

"He was just partying. Said life opened up for him on the beach yesterday. Wanted to get back to playing his music in front of people again. He was full of big plans. I was real tired. Couldn't stay up talking with him. Told him not to mix the booze and pills."

"What a good and true friend you had, Larry. Kenny was one of those people who didn't say a lot, but expressed his feelings and his friendship in his actions. He never left your side," said Hollywood.

"I won't leave his side either," said the fugitive. "Don't call hotel security or the cops. We'll get Kenny home ourselves."

The hotel staff looked on with bemusement as Larry and Teller rolled their wheelchair-bound friend through the lobby. Skinny Kenny wore Larry's sombrero, with the near-empty tequila jug cradled in his right arm.

"*Adios, amigos!* Had us a fine old time! Great country you got going here!" said Larry.

Convertible top up, they drove towards the Otay Mesa border crossing. Skinny Kenny lay across the back seat, sombrero and tequila bottle in place.

"Jesus, man—do you believe it? I'm supposed to be the ailing one, and Skinny goes and pulls this stunt," said Larry.

A police siren sounded; a motorcycle cop pulled them over.

"Just what we need," said Hollywood tensely.

"Be cool, now. Like in the movies," said Larry.

The cop appeared at the driver's window: aviator sunglasses, gold helmet, brass badge with LOPEZ engraved in black.

"You pass through stop sign, mister. Driver's license!"

"What stop sign?"

"The one you din see," said the cop through a mirthless grin.

Larry muttered under his breath.

"It's a shakedown."

Officer Lopez was just getting warmed up. "You want argue, we go to police station in Tijuana. Got a nice cell for you while we wait for the judge. But I think maybe he's on long vacation."

"My friend here's sick. We can't wait," said Teller.

"Pay fine now. A hundred dollars US."

Larry leaned over. "Officer?"

Lopez bent down and peered over to the passenger seat. Larry lifted up his shirt, exposing his skeletal frame, morphine pack, and the tubes disappearing directly into his chest. The officer was shaken.

"No, Señor! Put shirt down! Put it down! Fifty dollars."

Larry flashed a spectral smile. They paid the bribe and continued on their way back to the USA. On the other side. they finally relaxed.

"Lordy, Lordy—but I'm tuckered out," said Larry. He slept the remaining hundred and fifty miles home, awakening as the car engine intensified with the final climb up the mountain.

First stop: the Mountain Mortuary.

"Poor ole Skinny – it wasn't supposed to be him, now was it? But he went out on a high note. You know, this is the first time Skinny and I ever stepped foot outside the USA. At least he got to make some music on a sunny beach in old Mexico," said Larry.

"He was a great friend," said Hollywood.

"True gold in an untrue world..." said Larry.

Hollywood turned the battered convertible towards Kenny's house, where Larry would break the news to his wife.

"You know those TV shows *Roseanne* and *Married With Children?*" mused Larry. "Skinny and his old lady were like those crazy couples— arguing and yelling and misunderstanding—but underneath it all, there was this love..."

They pulled into a modest driveway.

Larry rang the doorbell then stood waiting, his friend's hat held discreetly behind his back. Kenny's wife opened the door with a big smile, which fell away at the sight of Larry's somber face, then dissolved into tears as Larry handed over her husband's hat.

Next, they arrived at Larry's twelve-year mountaintop refuge. "I gotta thank you, Hollywood. For the fun of it all. For making me feel like—a somebody," said Larry.

"Hey, you're the star of this project, my friend. If anybody should be giving thanks, it's me. We've got a movie on our hands!" said Hollywood. "We need to finish this puppy because I've already got our next project in mind."

"Another one? Go, Hollywood! What's the hook?"

"Two guys light out on a crazy whim to old Mexico and…"

"Love it already! Hey, where you overpaid Hollywood writers come up with your ideas anyway?" said Larry.

They cracked up. Larry's wife and two children were peering from the front window as the convertible pulled in. The family, reunited on their front porch, fairly glowed as the writer looked on from the car. Pam made her way over to the driver's window as Larry hugged his kids.

"Thank you so much," she said. "He's joyful. You gave him that. It's a blessing."

"We're all blessed by this, each and every one," said Teller.

Larry waved from the porch, beaming an everlasting smile and making a gracious bow.

It was the last time Hollywood would see his fugitive friend.

The End

… of the road.

MY HOBBY IS SILENCE

Last Chance for True Romance

This is a love story—with a difference. I can explain that differ-ence by telling you the kind of love story it's not, OK? It's not a love story tried and true, not meant to be, not at first sight, not two hearts beating as one, not May to September, not high school confiden-tial, not Romeo and Juliet, not Sampson and Delilah, not written in the stars or star-crossed—OK? Not your typical love story. So what kind of love story is this? What's left? Just Lola and me, that's what. Nothing more or less. Two people, two years. Got twenty minutes, Faithful Reader? Come along with us then...

From the tabloids and TV, you know Lola's been missing four months now, and the authorities have named me a "person of interest" in their investigation. You also know by now that certain sensational events have a way of following in my wake. What you don't know is the exact how and why of it all, the truth beneath the news stories. To those of you ready to put some effort into discovering the truth—God bless you and read on. I've lost everything and have nothing to hide or to gain except a sharing of the truth.

And so we begin. Years before Lola, there was Monique—one light-as-air feminine package floating down life's highway and straight into this hungry heart. We were small-town kids. I walked her to school and, yes, carried her books in those days before Kindles and iPads. We weren't boyfriend and girlfriend—somebody else had her hooks into me—but we sure took notice. Four years later, when we ran into each other in the city, that high school spark flared into a fire: a warm, then hot, then blistering fire! Oh yeah! I don't mean to brag but we made music like a pair of dueling violins. Simultaneous high notes—several times a night with words of love all the way from beginning to end. If you've been there, you know what I'm talking about. If you haven't, take my word for it: you need nothing more from this life. Monique and I had it all for six beautiful months—right up to the night I popped the question.

I made us a candlelit dinner at my place, complete with that Italian Chianti in the cool wicker basket. I learned to cook from my mother who passed on a thing or two before she walked out on the old man and me. The highlight of the meal was my homemade *crème brûlée* featuring a real diamond engagement ring right there inside the pudding. Romantic or what? Monique's big brown eyes popped!

"Sweet girl, will you be my wife?"

Instead of crying or shrieking or just saying, "Yes," Sweet Thing sat there in silence.

"Is something wrong?" I asked. More silence. "I didn't think it was such a bad offer," I joked.

She looked me over like an appraiser. "Gary, may I tell you something?" she said.

"Of course," replied The Fool. "No secrets here."

But sometimes secrets are a good thing. Sometimes they shield people from terrible truths. Sometimes people should keep their pieholes shut. This was one of those times. Monique told me she'd been having sex for money and gifts with different guys the past two years. This is how she paid cash for her BMW and how she was saving for a condo. This was her business plan until she reached her goals. Which made me kinda lucky to be getting it for free from her, she said. If I wanted to keep seeing her, and maybe take us on a Caribbean vacation, I could, but marriage was not in her cards.

"Sorry, Gary. Nothing personal." She slid the engagement ring back across the table.

"Nothing personal? Nothing personal!"

"Don't raise your voice to me. I'm just being honest. You're the one who said 'no secrets here.'"

Here's the thing: she allowed me no room for a normal reaction. No room for what the shrinks call "venting." I was more than pissed.

"Remember me, Monique? I'm the guy who said 'Will you marry me?' not 'Will you be my whore?!'"

She got to her cheating feet like she was the one who should be pissed.

The human body holds major reserves of adrenaline to help us run away from attacking bears and wolves and to help fight our fellow men to the death when necessary. Atop that human body sits a brain, whose job is to direct all that adrenaline. But sometimes the brain doesn't do its job—and the adrenaline just takes over. Right there in that low-rent love nest, that's exactly what happened: my adrenaline took over. And to our great, great surprise, I killed Monique. In less than thirty seconds. She liked designer scarves, and the one she was wearing doubled as a designer noose. Silk can do that. Those shiny strands spun by those hardworking Chinese worms are strong, man. Way too strong for anybody's good that night.

I was tried, convicted and went down willingly. Truly sorry for what I'd done. Fifteen years crawled by. Every one of those 5,475 days and nights, I dreamt of a new day dawning outside my prison of body and soul. My chance for freedom came one sunny afternoon with a new cellmate, in for armed robbery. With my history, he felt good bragging to me about a murder he'd never been fingered for. I would have kept his secret—prison code of honor and all—if the guy hadn't brushed his teeth like he did. And how was that? Like a garbage truck grinding its way down Main Street: loud, messy and disgusting.

"Jesus, man—you choking to death or brushing your teeth? Try switching to mouthwash."

"Can't hear you! Wait till I finish brushing my teeth!" He got off on bugging people. But he forgot you need to be careful with a cellmate. It's an intimate situation whether you want it to be or not.

"I'm not kidding here. It's really bugging me. Four times a day," I said.

"Chillin' with Mr. Dylan!" he said.

"What the fuck?" I said.

"Now you got it," he said.

OK. That's how you want it?

Eight weeks later, Mr. Colgate found himself back in court facing a first-degree murder charge with me the star witness. See how far that smile gets you now. I got early parole in exchange for my testimony—and something even sweeter. I got to meet Lola.

She was a reporter for *The Citizen*, assigned to city hall and the courts. She sat there in that press box during my cellmate's trial: beautiful, feminine, totally focused. Every day, she wore a new suit or dress, highlighting her long black hair, her too-big-to-be-believed eyes, and those perfectly sculpted upper arms of hers. Ever notice over the last 15 years or so the beautiful upper arm on a woman has become an endangered species? Thank you, McDonald's—*gracias*, Taco Bell. But Lola's—perfect! And those eyes—first time they met mine, I went swimming in them. Remember that old Hollies song, *Just One Look*? It happened during a recess.

"I'm Lola."

My guard stepped between us. "No direct contact with the prisoner."

Too late, goofball. Those beautiful big lamps of hers were shining directly on me. "We've got to stop meeting this way," I deadpanned.

She beamed. We were goners.

On the way back in the prison bus, my guard got his digs in. "How do you do it, man? I hit the clubs most weekends. Half the time, I can't even get them onto the dance floor. You show up in leg irons and orange polyester, and they throw themselves at you."

"Wanna trade places?" I said.

"I just want some of your mojo."

"Can't help you. Guards aren't tragically romantic," I said.

She wrote; I answered. My conviction was a matter of public record, so she knew everything about me. Didn't matter to Lola. Or maybe it did matter to her in a way I never fully understood. I was just grateful. Weekends she visited; something my parents never did. Our conversations were non-stop and totally honest, right down to the story of her failed marriage, her wonderful parents and sisters, my early years, the pitfalls of hopeless romance—Goddamn, after fifteen years of dating Rosy Palm, I had myself a real live girlfriend!

As the trial unfolded, our hungry eyes feasted on each other in our wood-paneled rendezvous. That courtroom was as romantic as any French restaurant or nightclub you might imagine. Our special place. When Mr. Colgate's guilty verdict came down, Lola and I were sorry to see it all end. But a month later, I was on parole, out after fifteen years, and in with my sweetie. Banner across the living room wall: WELCOME HOME, BABY. Balloons, champagne, chocolates, a five-course home-cooked meal, red rose petals strewn across the bedspread. It was all too much. Tears streamed down my face. She brushed them aside and kissed them away. No man was ever more blessed.

She couldn't bring herself to tell her old man what I'd done time for—didn't want him worrying. He was a nice old gent. Said his daughter and I made a really handsome couple. I don't mean to brag, but he wasn't the only one who said that.

Lola said I'm her Brad Pitt—just wish I had his bank account! Anyway, her dad offered me a job as a waiter at his restaurant, but I'm a little too independent for that line of work: "Hi. I'm Joe Dork and I'll be your waiter today. Let me tell you about our specials." No thanks.

But the old boy was good enough to front me a little cash for a second-hand truck and some painting equipment, and before you knew it, I was back in my old line of work as a painting contractor. I started with his house—didn't want to take any payment from him, but he insisted. People say I'm a natural salesman, and I guess they're right. Here's the thing: believe in yourself, sell yourself, and the deals will follow. Pretty soon, I had a stack of contracts and deposit checks, thanks to Craigslist. What a cool concept that Internet is!

Lola and I? Three months of total sexed-out bliss until I started asserting a little normal male independence. No women on the side or anything like that, just slipping away for a few hours to smoke a little weed, maybe pop a pill or two with some new friends. Just trying to relax, that's all. I'm not the kind of guy to join Rotary. Sorry, that's not me. But a guy still needs to get outta the house now and again. Know what I mean? Of course you do. But Lola?

"Why don't we stay in tonight, Gary? A little wine, some Netflix…" she said.

"Wasn't that last night?" I said. "Look, I got a problem about being cooped up—you understand…"

Fifteen years inside—who wouldn't understand? Lola, that's who. She wanted me all to herself.

"Sorry, Babe. I'm nobody's prisoner anymore," I said.

She also wanted me to start paying her old man back his loan right away. Sure, but give a guy a chance. It's not easy managing painters and plasterers—they're basically a bunch of drunks who take occasional time off from boozing to do a little work. Managing those guys is like herding cats. Then Lola got the bright idea she oughta keep the books and manage the money.

"But I've already got a parole officer," I said.

"Very funny," she said.

"About as funny as that leash you're trying to put on me," I said.

Then we had a real problem. I paid her old man back $2,000 of what I owed him. Then he tells Lola behind my back that two nights before—the night he had us over to his place for dinner—somebody stole $3,500 cash he took home from the restaurant and stashed in his upstairs bathroom.

"What's he trying to say, Lola? I stole his stash on a piss break upstairs, then gave it back to him as a loan repayment next day?"

"Of course not! Dad said no such thing!"

"Then why are we talking about it?" I said.

"I'm sharing something with you—my father's upset!"

"He's not the only one! I came out of a den of thieves but I'm no thief. Mine was a crime of passion. I'm not passionate about money—never have been. But your father? He's a businessman, right? Those dudes are all about the dollar. Making it. Keeping it. Why didn't he deposit that $3,500 in the bank? Concerned about taxable income?"

That slowed her down. "Let's just forget it, Babe," she said.

She seemed to mean it. But in the weeks to come, she let that cloud of suspicion hang heavy over my head. The dinner invites from Pops stopped. I started kicking back more with my new friends. And back home, the sex started fading. One night when I was in the mood, she just laid there, eyes closed, completely motionless while I did my thing. It really bugged me.

"Lola, next time if I want to do the wild thing with a stiff, I'll ask the local undertaker to fix me up. You stay out of it."

"That's disgusting! How can you say such a thing?" she said.

"How could you do such a thing?" I said.

Her beautiful left eyebrow arched up all mean and nasty. "You don't love me the way I need to be loved," she said.

"Take that leash off me and you'll see some love."

Women exert big power over men, and half the time they don't even know it. My own mother could torpedo your day with a goddamn raised eyebrow. Now here it was all over again.

"Lola? You hearing me? Nothing's perfect. Including this perfect life you've set up for us. Relax. Stop trying to control everything."

She could be hard of hearing when she wanted to be.

A few nights later, I returned home with a nice buzz going to find her all dolled up, down to her blue high heels.

"Somebody's looking hot," I said.

Silence. It turned out she was leaving for the evening to visit an "old friend." When I asked what friend, she got shifty and admitted it was an old boyfriend.

"So invite Mr. Wonderful over here," I said.

"There's too much tension in this house," she said.

"I don't like it—you heading into the night like this."

"Now who's trying to put a leash on who?" she said through a cute smile.

Off she went. A week later she started pulling the same move again, just like the first time. It tore me up again, and I told her so. "Lola, I've got a really bad feeling about that guy you're going to see. He's a loner, on his own in an isolated old farmhouse outside the city. Just the kind of guy you can't trust or predict. You're putting yourself into danger. Why would you want to leave somebody that loves you to spend time with that creep?"

"Ha! That's exactly what people said about you. I'm a big girl. I'll make my own decisions, thank you."

That was the last time I saw my honey.

I awoke to an empty bed, called her cell. No answer. Then her work. Then her old man. Finally, at 7 p.m., the Mounties. Now if your wife or girlfriend disappeared from home and got you sick worried, would the Mounties come down on you like an invading army? Not likely. It's a free country, and people move about it freely. But try being an ex-convict on parole for murder—the "ex" disappears, and you're a speck of dirt under a police microscope. That girl was the love of my life, my angel, my benefactor, all rolled into one. Her disappearance sent me to the bathroom every couple hours to throw up. I went on TV, gave newspaper interviews, passed out missing person flyers with her picture at intersections, co-operated fully with those salaried sons-of-bitches Mounties in their Boy Scout uniforms. They treated me like dirt. Even when they found her abandoned car near the farmhouse where her "old friend" was holed up.

"How about taking him in for questioning?" I asked the Mounties.

"Thanks for the hot tip, asshole. How about confessing?" they said.

Guess what, Sherlock? No body, no crime—just a missing persons case. My search for Lola continued. For four months. Then one morning, I got a call.

"I'm very sorry for your loss. I've been watching you on TV, listening to you on the radio. You're a good grieving man." The voice was kind. "I can help find her—if you're ready," she said.

She was a psychic with a file of press clippings and testimonials to prove it. She was also one of the very few from the past four months to show any real concern for my feelings. I invited her into our home.

"I love her so much," I said.

"I don't doubt that for a minute, Gary. That's why I'm here," she said.

"I have no money. Nobody answers my contractor ads now. I can't pay you."

"This is not about money," she said. "I'm here to help."

I've always had good instincts about people—this person I trusted.

"What do you need from me?" I said.

"Some personal objects of Lola's. Clothes, footwear, a favorite childhood toy. And a recent photo."

I obliged her.

"Now think back—what was Lola wearing when she walked out that door?"

I told her right down to the pink mittens and cashmere scarf I gave her for Christmas.

"I need to return home with Lola's things and retire early. In the morning, we set out to find your love."

"Are we going to the airport? Driving to another city?" I said.

A sudden sadness came over her.

"I can't be sure—but we'll start closer to home," she said.

I showed her to the door. Then the tears flowed, just like that magical afternoon when my honey first brought me home. Suddenly, through the fog of grief, a powerful idea emerged: an idea that could lead us straight to Lola's killer.

Next morning, we drove in the direction of that "old friend's" farmhouse. The psychic held a tattered teddy bear in her lap—a precious relic from Lola's childhood.

"I hope you don't mind—it helps establish a connection with her," she said.

It was oddly comforting. Then I laid my idea on her.

"That 'old friend' Lola was heading to see? Guy's a real loner—no wife, no kids. Lives on his own in a farmhouse."

We had left the city behind and were heading up into ski country.

"The newspaper said you went out there and confronted him," she said.

"You bet! I've seen loners just like that when I was inside. I told the Mounties he's probably holding her prisoner in an underground vault in his house or somewhere on his property. They wouldn't take me seriously—wouldn't even look into it."

"I take you seriously," she said.

We approached the spot where Lola's abandoned Camry was found.

"I'm starting to feel something now. Turn down that road," she said, pointing ahead to the left.

I turned onto an abandoned logging road that dead-ended after several hundred yards.

"Do you feel anything?" she said.

I shook my head. I began backing us out to the highway.

"I'm getting a vibe now that Lola is alone. And shivering. Not a good vibe," she said.

"Maybe that sonofabitch didn't hold her at his farmhouse after all," I said.

We headed a mile further down the highway then turned onto another abandoned logging road at her suggestion. No luck. I backed out onto the highway. "Let's try that one up ahead," I said.

This was the shortest of them all, no more than a hundred yards. We came to the end.

"Shall we get out and walk?" she said.

I opened my door. A grove of beautiful blue spruce beckoned. Something about them...

"Are you all right?" she said.

I had no words.

"We can call it a day and return tomorrow," she said.

"There's no tomorrow in this place," I said.

We walked towards the spruce grove, stooping under the low-hanging boughs, continuing towards a small clearing up ahead: a peaceful sorta spot. Fat white clouds floated overhead against a clear blue sky— a sky denied me for fifteen years. My guide stopped in her tracks. She was peering at something on the ground just up ahead...

"I'm so sorry," she said.

Fifteen minutes later, we made our way—still shaking—back down the logging road to the highway.

"You saw her final moments, her final resting place in your mind's eye before we got to it. You must have seen the sonofabitch who was with her—who did this to her," I said.

"Just a shadow…" she said.

"We can go to his farmhouse right now! Seeing him will fill in those shadows! Try! The police will listen to you," I said.

"I'm sorry but I'm just not feeling that vibe right now. Perhaps in the morning after I've slept on it, dreamt on it," she said.

"He's just a couple miles up the road," I said.

"I'll come by your apartment first thing in the morning; we'll confront him then."

The knock on my front door came early—6 a.m. It was harder and louder than I expected.

"You're under the arrest for the murder of Lola Ellis," said the flat-footed horseman. For me, those Mounties aren't the good guys: they're the Horsemen of the Apocalypse.

"You've nothing to hope for from any promise or favor and nothing to fear from any threat—"

"Save the speech, Sherlock. I've heard it before…"

"—anything you say can be used as evidence."

There they stood in their Boy Scout uniforms: smug on the outside, smirking on the inside.

Lola's case went from missing persons to first-degree murder because of that psychic who'd been working with the horsemen from day one. Sure had me fooled. It all came out in the charges they've filed. She's worked with them on missing persons cases before. Claims I led her to the body because I subconsciously felt deep guilt. Bullshit! Trumped-up Mountie bullshit! But what's it matter? I'm innocent and will be proven so in that same courtroom where Lola and I fell in love. How can I be so sure? Look at the facts. No witnesses to her murder. No evidence placing me at the scene of her remains. No physical evidence at our home. No blood, no clothing, no fibers, no tire tracks. No third-party alibi for her "old friend" placing him at home the night she disappeared. The police need to focus on that psycho, not me. I am the wrong man with the wrong record in the wrong place at the wrong time. But that doesn't make me guilty of murder. All it makes is a reasonable doubt.

And most important of all is this diary, written in my own hand and given to my friend—just before my arrest, with instructions to hand it over to my lawyer the second the Mounties haul me in. Which of course they now have. I knew they would, you see. I know them too well.

Dear Reader, lose no sleep over me. I am not afraid. I entrust this— the true story of Lola and me—to the care of my public defender and the twelve men and women who soon will sit in judgment on me. I have revealed everything, held back nothing. Yes, I have not always been an innocent man. But today, I am. And I will not allow my truthful words in this diary to be twisted by the Mounties and prosecutors, whose main mission is pursuing guilty verdicts. How many "killers" have lately been freed from death row based on newfound evidence? Behind every wrongful conviction are an overzealous cop and prosecutor. This precious diary will answer the prosecution's lies.

From this day forward, my hobby is silence. I will not be interrogated. I will not be examined by any prison shrink. I will not take the stand to be cross-examined by clever prosecutors. I will not meet the press. My hobby is silence.

I have now spoken—said my piece. I know my jury will see this diary for what it is—the sworn testament of an innocent man whose greatest crime has always been just loving too much.

Thank you. May God bless you and guide your deliberations.

APPENDICES: Newspaper Clippings

DOUBLE MURDERER CONVICTED: DNA EVIDENCE KEY
Two months later:
KILLER SLAIN BY FORMER CELLMATE: OLD SCORE SETTLED

... of the lies.

HOLLYWOOD CONFIDENTIAL

Saulie's Secret

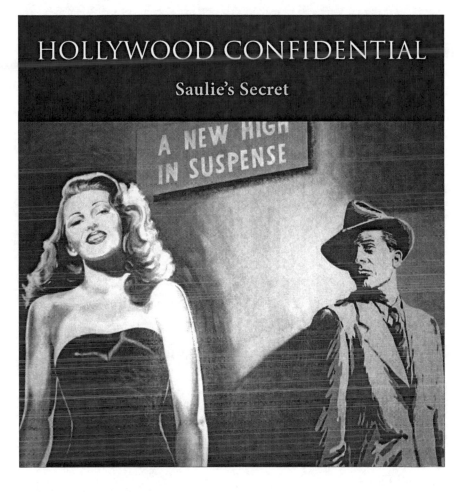

Teller arrived from afar in Hollywood with a high-concept movie proposal that sold for a six-figure amount. The president of the studio made the commitment on the spot in his prairie-sized office immediately after the story pitch, unaware this was the last of eight pitches Teller and his producer, Saulie, had been shopping around town. They had run out of energy, studios, and almost out of hope. Finally, miraculously, they had a sale.

"Didn't I tell you from day one—don't worry about it!" Producer

Saulie, a fast talker with a Hollywood track record, was exultant. "Didn't I tell you we'd sell this thing no problem? It's the '90s, baby, and we're hitting off the decade with a home run!" They were on the post-meeting elevator.

"Thanks, Saulie," the writer beamed. "But couldn't we have started here, instead of schlepping it all over town?"

"Hey, Baby—this is Hollywood! It's all about the drama," said the producer.

An associate producer named Furey had set up the meeting that sold the project. At the eleventh hour, he got brought on board by Saulie, who mentioned just two things to the writer: Furey was a "character," and he golfed with the studio president.

"Guys, tonight we celebrate at Luigi's! Bring your best ladies," said Furey.

Saulie begged off. "Sorry, can't make it—my machine gun's in the shop. But say hello to the GoodFellas for me, will you?" He laughed.

"Easy with the stereotypes, Saul. It's a great Italian restaurant, that's all," said Furey.

Teller and his wife drove up to Luigi's valet service ten minutes early. "I'm starving!" she said.

"What else is new?" he said.

Financial anxiety and the resultant overeating had altered her profile since they arrived in Hollywood eighteen months ago. A diminutive Ecuadorian valet opened the tattered convertible's passenger door. "Welcome to Luigi's."

They emerged into a balmy spring evening. The Santa Ana winds were blowing steadily in from the desert, bending the palm trees along Santa Monica Boulevard. A doorman smiled, bowed and ushered them into a seventies time warp.

Red leather, semi-circular button-back booths, southern Italian music in the spaghetti-scented air, solemn waiters in formal attire, a sprinkling of enhanced bosoms and hairy chests giving life to the room. Associate producer Furey, flanked by his date, waved from a prime booth.

"There he is," said the writer.

"With his daughter?" hissed his wife.

Furey rose. "Look everybody: they're here! The creative genius—the man of the hour—and his lovely wife!" There was no mistaking the producer-ly charm, and the fact he was absolutely sincere when introducing his much younger girlfriend as Lambykins.

"My, what a beautiful necklace," said Teller's wife.

"Thank you!" said Lambykins. "Carlo gave it to me for my twenty-first birthday. He's so sweet I could eat him all up!"

"Lucky Carlo," said Teller.

"Is Lambykins a—nickname?" Teller's wife asked.

The producer took the question. "It's like 'Madonna' or 'Cher' or..."

"I think we get the idea," interjected the wife.

Lambykins and Carlo exuded a charming and utterly genuine post-adolescent bliss. The twenty-five-year age difference was purely external. The writer marked the producer as an immature striver driven by huge ambitions and sudden enthusiasms: emotional, unpredictable, quick to be friend or enemy.

"Nice restaurant, Carlo," said the writer. He needed to establish a rapport with this golf buddy of studio presidents.

"I'm dining here for years. Place was started by some fellas from Vegas looking to get a foothold in California. Just like you! Go West, Young Man! Go West! Right? Am I right?!"

"You're right," said Teller.

"Hello?! That's how I make my living—by being right! Was I right about your story? Hey? Was I right?!"

"You were right, all right," said Lambykins.

"Hello! Thank you!" said the producer. He turned to Teller's wife. "Your husband hit Hollywood with one helluva story—a true original! And it's gonna take us all on a ride to The Bigs. You know that, right? Studio's crazy about it. Already set aside a production slot and thirty mill in funding for next year. I'm not kidding!"

Teller's wife suddenly burst into tears. "What? I said something wrong?" said the producer.

"No—no…" she said. "It's just—it's been so hard this past year and a half—and all of a sudden it's like a dream coming true…"

"Don't cry, Honey," said the writer. "This is a brand-new day and the reason we came here in the first place."

The producer patted Teller's wife's hand. "Baby, I understand. When I blew into this town from Jersey, I couch surfed all over LA. Couldn't make rent for a year. Then things started happening for me. Your guy's got talent. He's an original. What rock did you find him under, hey?

Just kidding! But now it's all happening for you two just like it did for me. Believe it! Embrace it!"

Teller's wife dabbed at her smudged mascara.

"Us girls are going to freshen up!" said Lambykins.

The ladies departed for the Ladies as a Sicilian sommelier hovered into view.

"Cecilio, Cecilio! Pop us some Veuve Clicquot!' commanded the producer.

"I'm here all the time. The place is like home to me," said Furey. "Goddamn Saulie refuses to set foot in here! Rather play kiss ass with some flavor-of-the-month actor or director at The Palms or The Ivy."

"Have you fellows produced together before?" said Teller.

"First time. You and your story are the glue, Kid."

"Saul has some major credits. That's why my agent sent me to pitch him," said Teller.

"Saulie's got the credits all right. And a dry spell going back three years. He needs a green light as much as the rest of us. And with your story and my buddy in charge at the studio we've got it!"

Uncertainty banished; prayers answered. California dreaming in real time. Producer Furey went suddenly somber.

"You heard what happened to Saulie a couple years back, didn't you?" he said.

"No."

"OK. Don't freak now, 'cause it was total trumped-up bullshit, and Saulie was acquitted by the jury," said the producer.

Silence descended.

"Acquitted of what?" said the writer.

The producer looked Teller dead in the eye.

"Not that..." said the writer.

The producer continued. "Saulie's dating this blond bombshell who's separated from her husband. Saulie's crazy about her. I mean totally nuts. Trouble is, so was her husband. One night, he beats Saulie up bad—sends him to emergency. Six weeks later, the jealous hubby turns up dead on the sidewalk in Bev Hills. Single shot to the back of the head. Professional job."

"Jesus!" said Teller.

"Easy, now," said the producer. "Saulie's a pussycat. A Hebrew pussycat. Those guys don't go around whacking people. Too messy. They use lawyers instead. Am I right? I'm right. Dead guy had plenty of enemies, believe me. Remember—Saulie walked outta that court a free man."

The writer absorbed it. "Thanks for filling me in," he said.

"You're entitled. Best you hear it from me." said Carlo. "Just don't get in any arguments with Saulie, OK? Guy's got a temper."

Dark humor on a sunny day. The blood drained from Teller's face.

"Hey, I'm kidding! C'mon!" said the producer, laughing.

"What about Saulie and the blond bombshell? Are they still together?" said Teller.

"Negatori, *muchacho*. This is Hollyweird! Blondie left Saulie for some guy with a bigger dick and a fatter bank account. Now there's a movie! How about we pitch that one to Saulie? The sequel to HARRY

MEETS SALLY—call it SALLY DITCHES HARRY!" Furey broke into uncontrolled laughter as the ladies returned.

"The powder room's entirely white! Italian marble! It's beautiful..." said his wife.

"That's nice," said Teller. He let Saulie's secret stay that way.

The writer began working on the all-important first draft, buoyed by the studio's commitment and their $100,000 first payment. Under his contract, he did a first draft and second draft for $100,000 each, and a polish for $50,000—all on a ninety-day schedule. As an established producer, Saulie stood to make $500,000 plus points when the movie was made, while Furey as the studio president's golf buddy had been favored with a $250,000 deal, generous for a producer with no credits.

Furey was a good golfer, and golf had been good to Furey. He made his business contacts at the Riviera Golf and Country Club—studio brass, actors, agents, investors—the buyers and sellers of the film business. He was a golf buddy of a major movie star, offering good cheer and sophisticated golf tips. He helped him break ninety on the world-famous Riviera course and then work his way down into the low eighties. In return, the star favored him with invitations to parties at his home on Mulholland Drive, plus the occasional Lakers game in his courtside seats. Furey was known on the A-list fringe of the film business, but harbored a deep longing for a production credit—to one day ride that fierce breathing beast that was an A-list Hollywood movie in production. Teller learned it all over lunch with Saulie at The Palm Restaurant in West Hollywood.

"Furey knows everybody at Luigi's," said the writer.

"Crowd's hipper at this place. Big film industry hangout. Luigi's is an old mob joint bankrolled by guys kicked outta Vegas," said Saulie.

"C'mon!" said the disbelieving writer.

"It's true. Check the pictures on the walls next time you're there. And Furey knows all those mob guys—he's from Jersey. That's how we met. He came and pitched me this movie idea about a gangster saga spanning three generations. He wanted to write and direct it but the guy's no writer and certainly no director. I liked his idea, offered to co-produce with him. But by the time he started backing off the writer-director thing, it was too late. Francis Ford Coppola announced a little project called *The Godfather*. We're left at the station waving bye-bye."

"Is our Furey connected to those mob guys?" said the writer.

"People say he knows people. But you never heard that from me," said Saulie. "Look, I'm being up front because I don't want you worrying about any crap you might hear about Furey. I ran a background check on the guy before doing our co-producer deal. Clean as a whistle. No problem."

Teller was left to digest the fact his producers were, according to their own descriptions of each other, jury-acquitted and mob-connected. In the end, he concluded such Hollywood color really didn't concern him; he pushed it to the back of his mind and got on with the writing. Six weeks later, he submitted the all-important first draft. The studio liked the script, but had eight pages of detailed notes and suggestions for the writer.

"No problem! Studio wants some changes, you give them their changes," said Saulie.

"A lot of notes there—very picky," said the writer. It was his first studio experience.

"Think of it like tailoring a fine suit," said Saulie. "They bought your design—you went to your workshop and made up the first fitting—now they want a few alterations. Big deal. I'm telling you, no problem. Don't worry about it!"

Another day in the movie business. Furey was similarly positive. "You're on third base, kid. All you gotta do is steal home. Saulie and I are here at home plate cheering you on. We got ourselves an A movie!"

Three weeks later, a second draft was submitted to the studio, and writer and his producer found themselves back at Luigi's.

"I've got big, big news for you," said Furey.

"Your golf buddy's read the script?" said Teller.

"Bigger: I've decided to direct the picture."

Teller's adrenaline spiked. "What? Have you spoken to Saulie, to the studio?" he said.

"I'm telling you first, out of respect for you as the creator of this wonderful project."

"Well, thank you, but…"

"You're welcome! I believe in this 1,000 per cent. I've already got it cast in my head!" said Furey.

"But first the studio has to green-light the project, then they choose the director. Isn't that how it works?" said Teller.

"They're gonna love the script. Their story notes were positive. As for the director—who approves him? My golf buddy at the top who gave us our development deal. Hello?! Am I right?"

The writer slid from the booth and pointed towards the washrooms. "Excuse me," he said.

Inside the white marble sanctuary, he made a quick call. "Saulie, the guy wants to direct! He just told me."

"There he goes again! Crazy fuck glory hound. Studio will never buy that. Let me handle this. I know what to do," said Saulie.

Teller splashed cold water on his face, suddenly adrift on the ever-shifting sands of Hollywood. Exiting the washroom, he faced a wall of photographs of celebrity visitors to Luigi's: second-tier actors, a smattering of grinning singers and someone familiar: Furey, arm in arm with an anonymous forty-something stranger in an expensive suit. He returned to their booth.

"Saw your picture back there."

Furey smiled. "My fifteen minutes of fame."

"Who's the guy you're with?"

Furey chuckled. "A connected fella. Does a lot of work for the owners of Luigi's. Legal and personal issues. Solutions to problems. I fixed Saulie up with him awhile ago. You ever come up against a problem you can't cope with—come to me, OK? Every problem has a solution, believe me."

"I'll keep that in mind," said Teller.

"So you should. We're partners, right?" said Furey.

A week later Saulie called. "Meet me at The Palm in an hour."

They convened in his reserved booth.

"The studio got back to me this morning on our project," said Saulie. "This is the worst goddamn day of my freakin' life. The worst!"

"They don't like my second draft?" asked Teller.

"They like it fine. Want a few more tweaks—nothing major. We got a bigger problem. I cannot convince Furey to back down on the director thing and I know from the get-go the studio will never turn over a $30-million picture to a first-time 45-year-old wannabe director—even if he does play a good golf game. Idiot!"

The writer pondered. "OK. So now you need to meet directly with the studio, right?"

Saulie hesitated.

"I don't know about that. Studio's his relationship. Furey'd go ballistic if I went to them. He could do anything, even bad-mouth me to the studio president. Anything!"

The writer smelled the fear bubbling up in Saulie.

"And now the crazy fuck has threatened to take the project to the other studios if ours won't let him direct."

"Those other studios already turned us down," said Teller.

Saulie's face was turning an ominous color. "It's been three years since I've had a green light! You know how hard it is to get a film studio-approved? The odds are off the chart. Everybody in this goddamn restaurant including the waiters would give their left nut for a movie deal! And this idiot's letting his ego fuck it up? He's absolutely nuts! Unbelievable!" Saulie was shaking with rage. "And he says he's going to sue me if I don't back him up. Says we're partners, and I have a fiduciary obligation to him as my partner."

"Partnerships work in both directions," said Teller.

"Not with him! How far did they get reasoning with Napoleon or Hitler?"

The writer pondered the politics.

"Go directly to the studio president and tell him you don't support Furey as director. Tell the president they need to draw the line with this guy," said the writer.

Something was holding Saulie back.

"There's another way," said Saulie. "There are three of us involved here—you, me and Wingnut. You gotta make a choice. Who you gonna ride with? The third guy will be odd man out. Stick with me. We'll partner up, just the two of us. Tell the studio you can't work with Furey any more. He's giving you bad story advice, and his director ambitions are stupid. Cut Wingnut loose. Let him eat shit."

Saulie was clearly not about to go direct to the studio himself. It was as if Furey was holding something over his head.

"I need to think about this overnight, OK?" said Teller.

"Think clearly," said Saulie. "Remember: it's called Show Business— emphasis on the word 'business.' Studio's got a $30-million decision to make here. That's a whole lotta ass to cover."

Saulie was still talking as they waited outside for the valet. "I said this was the worst day of my life. The crap started flying before Furey called. At 6:30, I'm awakened by a goddamn floodlight in my eyes from the driveway next door. Bitch moved in there last month—up real early for work—still dark. Has this motion sensor floodlight on her driveway. I've asked her three, four times, very nicely, to please turn it off. This time I jump outta bed and hustle down to her driveway. Tap on her car window. She looks up at me like Ilsa the storm trooper and says: 'Yes? May I help you?' Bitch *knows* she's driving me nuts every morning before dawn and all she can do is ask if she can *help* me?" Saulie was shaking and reddening all over again. "It was all I could do to stop myself from reaching through her car window and wringing that scrawny bitch neck of hers! I'm telling you, man—bitch came closer than she'll ever know..."

Teller's mind was racing. If Saulie could get this furious at being awakened by a neighbor's floodlight, what level of anger would a jealous husband attacking him and sending him to emergency provoke? Enough to kill? And who exactly was the mysterious man with Furey in the photo at Luigi's? Furey's mob connection who hooked Saulie up with a hit man? Was this the true bond between the oddly mismatched producer duo? If so, Furey totally had the goods on Saulie and could open the gates to prison with a phone call. The writer was living a real-life movie within a movie in development.

Saulie's blue Rolls pulled up.

"Nice wheels," said Teller.

"You'll have one of your own soon enough, kid. Let me know your decision. Think clearly."

And he was gone.

The writer made a crucial call from his car. "How can you be so sure the studio will let you direct?" he asked.

The voice on the other end overflowed with confidence. "You want gray hair, kid? Stop worrying! Studio president's my golfing buddy. Friend of ten years," said Furey.

"He lets all his golfing buddies direct movies?" said the writer.

"You're funny! Such a talent. Listen to me—directors are a dime a dozen in this town. There are a couple dozen guys who could handle this picture—better me who's been there from the beginning and truly believes in it. But great scripts like yours—diamonds!—very rare. Screenplays are what drive this business, kid. Stop obsessing. This deal is screenplay-driven and it's done!"

Teller's choices were starkly clear: an acquitted killer with a solid Hollywood track record, or a mob-connected aspiring director with a studio president for a friend. Nothing in his Writer's Guild contract covered this.

"Just make it all happen, Furey," said the writer, sounding suddenly weary.

"Don't worry about it!" said the ever-chipper voice on the other end.

Six nights later, Teller received a midnight call from Palm Springs.

"I'm with Lambykins holed up five days at the Four Seasons. Haven't shot a round of golf, haven't shaved. Getting all our meals from room service."

"You'll wear that poor girl out," said Teller.

"No! I'm here for work. Punching up your script, doing a director's polish. Making it more visual, cutting dialogue, making our hero more heroic—giving him some big moments. He gets decorated by the President, wins a triathlon, that sorta thing. You're gonna love what I'm doin'!"

Teller plopped down. "But he's not the heroic type. He's no

Superman or Batman or Spiderman. Just an everyday Joe who, in spite of himself, steps up big-time and does what needs doing. That's who he is and that's the true power of the story," said the writer.

"Yeah, yeah. What you wrote is great, kid. I'm just taking it to the next level, that's all," said Furey.

"Would you mind telling me what you've written before?" said the writer.

Furey's charm gave way to immediate irritation, as the writer knew it could from day one.

"Hey—you worry too much for a young man! This movie's getting made. I'm just showing you a little respect by keeping you informed! This project is gonna change your life. It's gonna make you. This is day one of the Hollywood career you were born for. Don't worry about it!"

The line went dead.

As did the movie. Saulie transitioned to other studio projects, Furey returned to golf, **and Teller moved on with a more seasoned view of his adopted City of Angels**.

The End

… of a Tinseltown tug-of-war.

ONE ROOM HONEYMOON

Old Reunion and New Union

Once upon a time in small-town Nova Scotia, the boys were the fastest of friends—the acknowledged leaders of the A **class,** the academically gifted who were encouraged to discuss English literature and conjugate French and Latin verbs, which would somehow lead to lofty faraway opportunities their beloved hometown could never offer them. **High school as flight school.** In their senior class yearbook, Andrew was voted "cleverest" and "most likely to succeed,"

while Lee was "most popular" and consistently elected to student council—though never its president, as Andrew liked to remind him. Outside class, they strove to amuse and outdo each other. That last hometown Halloween, they sat on Lee's front porch, tossing firecrackers onto Dominion Street. The pile of combustibles behind them suddenly ignited, bringing Lee's mild-mannered father at the gallop with a water bucket. They had steady girlfriends—Andrew's smart and sexy, Lee's cute and a "good head," though not in the modern sense of the word. One couple had passionate teenage sex and kept it their small-town secret, while the other petted heavily and joked a lot. Sex and near-sex. Finally, in the fall of their eighteenth year, they departed the old hometown forever—for separate universities and separate lives unlinked by cell phones, e-mail, or Facebook.

Seven years later found the old friends together again in their nation's cold capital: Lee pursuing a comfortable career with the federal government, Andrew starting a record company specializing in comedy and children's albums. Lee was the first to buy a house.

"You got the jump on me, old buddy," said Andrew. "Nice house, cute girlfriend, home cooking, someone to laugh at your lame jokes—good job!"

"Don't go getting all envious," said Lee. "You think it's domestic bliss? Not totally."

"How so? Jane's got a great figure, always laughing, nice to your friends—what's the issue?" said Andrew.

Lee delivered the news like a small-town broadcaster. "Jane is very self-centered. She doesn't really care about her fellow man."

"Fellow man? Meaning you, old buddy?" said Andrew.

"Meaning mankind in general. All of us. Jane has no altruism. Last week, I brought this old guy—OK, this old drunk—home from the Bytown Tavern. He needed a place to sleep. Used to be a car dealer, down on his luck—so I invited him back to crash on our couch. Jane displayed no interest in the guy whatsoever. Next morning, she makes this cold breakfast—our guest asks for bacon and eggs. Jane takes me aside, tells me he has to go, said he smelled..."

"Did he?" asked Andrew.

"OK. Maybe a little but he's homeless, you have to make allowances—and even the Salvation Army serves a hot breakfast..."

"Jesus, Lee! You bring a smelly bum home from the tavern and expect your girlfriend to treat him like family? Come on! It's her home, too!"

"Not for long," said Lee. "I'm putting the house up for sale, quitting Jane and the government and moving in with you. I'll pay half the rent, sweep up and take out the garbage; you do the cooking and wash the dishes. I can't stand washing dishes."

"Say what?!" said a wide-eyed Andrew.

The roommate arrangement worked surprisingly well. Andrew spent his days in the recording studio and his office growing his music business, while Lee smoked enormous quantities of weed at his writing desk, pounding out his first novel.

"What's it all about?" said Andrew.

"Sharing. The importance of sharing," said Lee.

"OK, Gandhi. But could you be a little more specific? Like—sharing what? Perhaps I could read a few pages?"

"That's one thing I'm not quite ready to share," said Lee.

His inquisitive friend persisted.

"You think I'm trying to mess with your mojo, old buddy?" said Andrew. "I work with artists every day at the studio. They all think they shit Picassos. And I'm happy when they do. I'm on your side. Just curious, that's all"

"I'm curious, too," said Lee. "To see if I could borrow your car tomorrow. Got a few errands to run. I'll return it with a full tank of gas."

Lee had a way with surprise proposals. No matter: it was a brand-new Volvo, not something Andrew was inclined to lend.

Two weeks later, Lee raised another sharing-related issue.

"I can't keep up with your consumption," said Lee.

"What consumption?" said Andrew.

"The toilet paper, the orange juice, the string cheese, my Oreos. I'm writing, I'm smoking up, I get the munchies, I need my Oreos!"

Eight weeks later, they went their separate ways—Lee to a rooming house to finish his novel, Andrew to Los Angeles to pursue his dreams in the music industry.

Twenty years rolled by. They kept in intermittent touch, linked by e-mail and increasingly ancient history. Lee stuck diligently to his writing, completing seven unpublished manuscripts he insisted on calling "novels," while marrying a divorcee with a steady job and ready-made family. Andrew became prosperous, married, divorced, became more prosperous, then fell in love with a significantly younger woman.

Michelle brought enthusiasm and a slim waist to the relationship—two qualities that had gone missing from his first marriage. That she was blonde-haired, blue-eyed California gorgeous also didn't hurt. Their wedding would take place on the sunny sands of Santa Monica Beach, attended by the groom's Canadian and American friends and the bride's large California family. Lee was among the first to arrive.

"Pleased to meet me!" he exclaimed through his trademark loopy grin.

The small-town buddies hugged.

"Twenty years before you visit LA? What—I have to throw the party of the decade to pry you loose from your cave up there?" said Andrew.

"You haven't changed a bit!" said Lee. "Arrogant as ever!"

"Whatever happened to that sharing and caring thing you used to rave on about?" said Andrew.

"Still promoting that; one people, one world!" beamed the unperturbed Lee.

"You and Castro are just about the last ones signed up for that particular trip," said Andrew.

"Si, Señor!" said Lee.

Festivities began with a welcome barbecue for fifty at the groom's large California Craftsman home in trendy Venice Beach. The highlight of the house tour was a visit to the prairie-sized master bedroom and adjoining panic room.

"What's a panic room?" asked Lee of the Innocent North.

Andrew smiled. "If you hear an intruder downstairs, you just hop into the panic room. The door closes and locks automatically—sound-proof, burglarproof, bulletproof. Call Securicor on your cell—and wait for the cavalry to come to the rescue! My bride loves the security."

"I can use this in my new novel," said Lee. "LA Man, an entire new species—living on debit cards, sunscreen and panic rooms. Love it!"

Andrew didn't see the humor.

"At least I've been evolving, old buddy. Didn't let myself get stuck in some small-town time warp watching the world pass me by," Andrew said.

"Should I be taking notes?" said a grinning Lee. The man was unflappable.

Downstairs, Lee was meeting and greeting the bride and her bridesmaids.

"You're a writer," said the bride. "That's so interesting—so creative. Where do you find your ideas?"

"On my pillow in the morning," said the writer.

The ladies laughed.

"I'm getting seasick. Anybody got a barf bag?" said Andrew.

Lee's positivity was a hit with the ladies.

"Now you stop that, Grouchy!" admonished the bride. "Tell us, Lee—as Andrew's oldest friend here tonight..."

"Guilty!" interrupted Lee.

More laughter. Andrew rolled his eyes.

"What was my husband-to-be like back in high school? Tell the truth now!" she said.

Lee pondered. "My dear friend Andrew was—less evolved No chauffeur, no personal assistant, a small-town boy at heart…"

More chuckles.

"…but always ambitious. Couldn't wait to blast away from Canada and pursue a larger agenda."

"What are you writing at the moment, Lee?" asked a comely bridesmaid.

"A sequel to *Jurassic Park*. I'm presenting it to Spielberg tomorrow morning. Meeting him in my tux!"

"Wow! Good luck with that!" chorused the ladies.

"Thank you. Thank you very much," clucked Lee.

"Care to take a bow?" said Andrew.

As the evening wound down, Andrew and half a dozen old buddies gathered around an outdoor fire pit. The men—married and divorced—were offering the groom some last-minute counsel. The married ones were relaxed and supportive.

"She's young. She's beautiful. I hate your guts."

"Just remember your new two-word mantra: 'Yes, dear.'"

"Secret to a long, happy marriage: She can't get fat. You can't go broke. And most important of all: separate bathrooms."

His divorced buddies were more tentative.

"I really hope this works out for you."

"Got a good prenup?"

"Is she happy with the dog or does she want kids?"

Lee was in the first group. "Just do your best to make her happy, that's all. Be caring and sharing. You'll have a long happy life together," he said.

"Thank you, Dr. Phil, for sharing that sharing thing," said Andrew. "Remember when you and Jane broke up back in the day? You sold your house and gave her half, remember? You weren't even married. Why'd you do that?"

"The breakup was my idea. And Jane needed the money," said Lee.

"OK. Look—this wedding's costing me more than your little house was ever worth. I could use a little help with some bills right now. How about it?" said Andrew.

"When Spielberg snaps up my screenplay, no problemo!" said Lee.

Andrew looked at his old friend across the fire pit. "People think Hollywood's a dream factory. But this place has nothing on you, old buddy. You're a one-man fantasyland. Know what kinda gets to me, Lee? Your holier-than-thou sharing thing. But sharing what? Some unsold dreams and manuscripts? Hollywood's full of dreamers—occasionally they get lucky and sell something, or marry a rich divorcée, or more likely just head back to Toronto, Ontario, or Buttfuck, Ohio, when their debit cards go bust."

"C'mon, Andrew," said an old friend. "Lee flew all the way out here to support you on your big day. Take it easy."

A second friend weighed in. "He's probably gathering material for his next story. You better be nice!" he said.

Lee smiled.

The ceremony took place the following afternoon on Santa Monica Beach just before sunset. The bride, radiant in a Versace gown, was given away by her father. The best man was the groom's handsome 23-year-old son. The ceremony was followed by an outdoor semi-formal dinner for sixty, with waiter service and assigned seating. Andrew and his bride at the head table were distracted by a commotion at Lee's table.

"Excuse me a moment," said Andrew, getting to his feet.

Lee was attempting to seat a disheveled, poorly dressed woman.

"What's going on?" asked Andrew.

"This is my friend Mary. She needs a seat," said Lee.

"Come here a minute," said Andrew, drawing Lee aside. "What the hell are you doing? She's a bag lady, homeless."

Lee was unperturbed. "Mary is also very nice, very hungry, and my guest," he said.

"Oh—like the bum you brought home that night to Jane? You never learn, do you?"

"Mary is my guest," Lee repeated.

"No, she's not. You're the guest. She's the bum. Get her out of here right now, or I'll have security haul her away."

"Is it really so hard for you to share?" said Lee.

Andrew's expression said it all.

Lee returned to his table and offered his arm to his homeless friend.

"This way, Mary, my dear. There is a fine pizza parlour just up the street," he said.

"What's wrong with this place?" came the uncomprehending reply.

They left arm in arm. Several hours later, Lee returned to the newlyweds at the party. "Sorry about the seating mix-up—I think I overstepped my bounds," he said.

"That was no mix-up, Lee. Next time try being generous with your own hospitality, not somebody else's," said Andrew.

"Well said, old friend! I'll remember that! Live and learn!"

"You? You'll never change," said Andrew.

"Don't be a cynic! Never too late to see the light—let me prove it! You two are leaving in the morning on your honeymoon, right?" said Lee.

"Paris, Cannes, Venice and Vienna—a full month," said Andrew.

"Boy, do you know how to live, old buddy!" said Lee.

"No need to kiss my ass," said Andrew.

"Ha! Good one! Look—let me come by the house in the morning and make you guys a fantastic farewell brunch before you take off. I'll even see you into the limo and help with your bags."

"Lee—that's so sweet!" said Michelle.

Andrew looked at his old friend appraisingly. "Man, you're out of your freaking mind. You know that, right?"

Lee snapped to attention, saluting smartly.

"Guilty as charged!" he said.

The next morning at 10, Lee arrived at Andrew's carved walnut double door. "Old crony reporting for brunch duty!" he chirped into the intercom. Fifteen minutes later, he was preparing ham and cheese omelettes on the back patio as Michelle watched.

"This is majorly nice of you," said Michelle.

"Never too late to live and learn!" said Lee.

"Did you see Andrew's little honeymoon gift to the two of us?" she asked.

She brought Lee over to a cell charging station where a pair of diamond-encrusted iPhones sat in their docks.

"Wow!" said Lee.

"He's so romantic," said Michelle.

Andrew joined them. Lee began expounding. "In the next life, we're all going to end up in this great Heavenly army. Of course, we'll each be assigned a military rank and new name. Andrew's will be Major Romance."

"Such an imagination!" exclaimed Michelle.

"That's exactly what Spielberg's receptionist said to me yesterday!" said Lee.

"Barf bag! Barf bag!" said Andrew.

"So your big meeting went well?" Michelle asked, ignoring her husband.

"Totally! More news as it happens," said Lee. "Now what do you suppose my name and rank in the Heavenly army will be?" he asked.

"Oh, that's easy," said Michelle. "Sergeant Silly!"

Lee and the bride laughed like school kids as Andrew shook his head and checked his Rolex.

"Give me a hand with the bags, will you?" he asked Lee.

The three were in the master bedroom where the Louis Vuitton luggage awaited the journey to Europe.

"This is it? Everything we packed?" asked the groom.

The bride nodded. Lee stepped forward. "One last thing. That whole panic room feature you got going? Total bullshit. I can break through that system and get into that locked-down room in sixty seconds."

"The Hell you can!" said Andrew.

"A thousand bucks says try me!" said Lee.

Andrew was not a man to back down from a challenge, and his old friend knew it. "Lock yourselves in never-never land, and I'll have you out in under sixty seconds," said Lee.

Andrew set his Rolex Oyster chronometer.

"In 5-4-3…"

The newlyweds entered the panic room; the steel door thunked shut behind them. Lee paused, then waved jauntily at the peephole. He stepped out onto the upstairs landing, slid down the semi-circular oak banister to the main floor, then through the kitchen and out the patio door. He opened an electrical panel and tripped the master power switch, cutting off all electricity. He made his way over to the diamond-encrusted iPhones in the charger, ignited the gas grill beside it, and placed the phones on it. Then he made his way through the house and opened the front door to face a uniformed limo driver.

"I've been ringing the bell," said the driver.

"Short circuit," said Lee.

Lee stepped outside, closed the front door and picked up the suitcase he had left on the porch.

"I'll take that," said the driver.

"Thank you so much," said Lee.

"Beautiful home," said the driver, taking it all in.

"I like it. It's very comfortable," said Lee.

They passed through the front gate, which the driver bolted. Lee paused to peer up beyond the Securicor sign to the soundproof, bulletproof, reflective window of the panic room.

"One-room honeymoon!" he called out.

"What honeymoon?" asked the driver.

"Oh no, that's just the title of my next movie: *One-Room Honeymoon*. The long-awaited sequel to *Jurassic Park*. I'm the screenwriter."

"Really?! Terrific title, sir. Very intriguing. Everyone has a soft spot for honeymoons," said the driver.

"Thank you sooo much. I'm working with Spielberg. He's fast-tracking it. We'll be shooting by the fall. "

"Congratulations!" said the driver, well-schooled in the art of show biz flattery.

"I'm blessed. Steven's a pussycat," said Lee.

The driver held the door open. Lee ducked inside; they eased quietly away.

"If you don't mind my asking, sir, where do you writers come up with your fantastic ideas?"

Lee settled back for the ride to LAX. "My stories are all based on real life. People I meet, situations I encounter—I give them my own spin, of course… "

"Absolutely. So what kind of honeymoon is this one?" said the driver.

"Oh, a very intense one that puts our lovers totally to the test. To learn more, though, you'll need to buy a ticket."

The driver beamed from the rear view mirror. "Sold, sir! I'll be right there opening night."

"Excuse me, driver, I have to make an important call, 'Securicor? I have a service call for you. You can take care of it tomorrow, that would be fine.'"

"Can you say where your couple honeymoons?" interrupted the driver.

The writer's eyes twinkled devilishly. "Sorry—can't be spoiling the surprise for you."

"I understand, sir! You screenwriters—you love your surprise endings!"

"Indeed we do, driver." Lee gazed out at the palm trees floating lazily by. "Indeed we do. **This is Hollywood after all…**"

The End

… of a high school rivalry.

MOONWALKING
WITH MICHAEL

When Music Meets The Movies

I t was the best of times.

Teller and his son walked hand in hand down the palm-lined sidewalk to school at 7:30 each morning.

"Daddy, what kind of school did you go to in the olden days?" A blond seven-year-old fountain of questions.

"It was a small village, Son. School was just one big room. Each aisle a different grade." A latter-day hippie, California transplant, a screenwriter.

"One room? Little kids and big kids together all day, not just at lunch time?"

"Oh, yes."

"Sounds fun," said the boy.

"It was."

A hummingbird flitted by.

"Dad? Come to class with me today. There's an empty desk. Jackie Manning got kicked out for biting people."

"That's quite an offer, Son. Thank you very much. But I have work…"

"To make money?" said the boy.

Dad nodded.

"Don't worry. You can have my allowance. And if that's not enough we can open up my piggy bank."

"No need for that. A man must guard his piggy bank. "

The boy was undeterred. "You think the kids will tease you because you're big."

"Well—I am six feet tall."

"Dad—Tony Baloney in the eighth grade is bigger than you right now! We'll hang out with Tony at recess. "

"It sounds great—it really does—but…"

"I know! You're shy! You're alone all day writing and you're shy."

He pondered. "You may be on to something there."

"C'mon, Dad! At lunchtime, we're all together at the picnic

tables—tell your stories to the kids like you tell them to me at home—they'll like you, I promise!"

It was the best of times.

—⁕—

Twenty minutes later, he was at work in the writing studio in the back-yard of the small Venice Beach bungalow. Work began with *Night Court* on Fox TV—an ever-dependable source of squabbling local color. Suddenly a SPECIAL REPORT interrupted the program—a live aerial news report from a fast-food restaurant in south central LA. A famous rock star had given into the urge for a Big Mac and strolled into a McDonald's. Minutes later, a mob of fans surrounded the place, and the star had to be airlifted to safety. Another day in the wild, wild West—but a very special day for a certain screenwriter.

Teller drove down Santa Monica Boulevard to his agent's office. The agent: young, aggressive, calculatingly eccentric. He wore tailor-made orange suits and, of course, called himself Agent Orange. A younger, Day-Glo version of Colonel Sanders. The name had been ac-quired during his relocation from Hawaii to Hollywood. Through the Hollywood grapevine, the agent had come into possession of one of the writer's unsold spec scripts and loved it. He tracked the writer down, introduced himself on the phone and asked for a meeting. They were face to face the next day in the agent's office, surrounded by neat stacks of screenplays with the titles in Magic Marker along the bindings.

"I can't help wondering how many of those scripts got sold," said the writer.

"Never enough," said the agent. "But I've got twenty clients, and the majority are working under studio contracts right now. You should be one of them, Teller!"

"Why the name Agent Orange?"

"So they'll remember me, which helps me sell you."

That was three months ago: still no writing assignments. Today, it took fifteen minutes for the writer to pitch his new story; the reaction was swift.

"Jesus Christ, I sit here all year waiting for something like this!"

Agent Orange was practically levitating.

"You really think so?" said Teller.

"Top of my fucking head's blowing off!" said Agent Orange. "And your idea for who we pitch it to—I mean, Michael Jackson's only the biggest pop star in the world! If he goes for it, there'll be no stopping this thing."

The writer had never seen such excitement from an agent. Inspiration when it happened was a palpable thing.

"I hear he's interested in making the transition into the movies," said the writer.

"Not just interested," said Agent Orange. "Michael Jackson's got offices and a full development deal at Columbia. I had lunch with his director of development last week. You've gotta meet her—they haven't found a project yet. Man, when they hear this, they're gonna kiss my Hollywood ass! This project is going to make your career—this is one high-stakes game we're playing here. In case you didn't realize it, Teller, the fame game and the money game are totally linked. We get in business with Michael Jackson, and there's no looking back, my friend."

Forty-eight hours later, Teller passed security at the Columbia Studio gates, proceeded to the second floor of Bungalow 24, and entered a door simply marked MJJ PRODUCTIONS. Looking down from the reception room wall was a large framed photograph of the most popular singer in the world in full flight on stage. The receptionist noticed him noticing.

"I'm a huge fan," Teller said.

The door to an inner office opened and MJJ's director of development appeared—a vision in white: thirty-something, perfectly white complexion, white designer dress, white belt, white watch strap.

"I am *so* pleased to meet you," extending an almost translucent hand. "Michael calls me Missy." She led the way into her office, launching straight into the business at hand.

"I can't believe how hard it is to find an original idea in this town. Remakes, sequels, prequels, adaptations, translations. But original stories? Forget it. The easy part for me was landing the dream job; the nightmare is trying to find the right project."

"I understand you're not from the film industry," Teller said.

"Publishing. New York. Random House sent me to talk to Michael about a coffee table book on his concert performances. He wasn't keen. Turned out he had something else in mind for me. Here we are."

"What would Columbia like him to do?" he asked.

She smiled dismissively. "A remake or a sequel or an adaptation of any musical that's ever been made. But he's all about becoming a movie star—a legitimate actor. Not the lead in a musical. And he doesn't do remakes. Period. Michael creates; he doesn't remake."

"I heard Michael financed the *Thriller* video himself," said Teller.

"You've done your homework. The studio was ready to spend maybe $50,000 on a five minute video—what Michael had in mind was full-on feature quality, feature director, actors, sets—$500,000 for ten minutes. He paid for it; loved the shooting and editing process. The album broke all sales records largely because of the video."

Teller nodded. "Those scenes with him and the girl on the illuminated sidewalk and in the movie theatre? He was completely natural—relaxed. This guy can act," he said.

"Let's hear your pitch," she said.

The story had a one-word title: *Invisible*. It began with a madcap inventor—an unsuccessful version of young Thomas Edison. A university dropout with an irrepressibly fertile imagination, he lurched from idea to idea, none of which paid the rent. His latest invention was a cream that would remove unwanted tattoos—no more painful medical removals or skin grafts. He applied the potion to a tattoo on his own upper right arm. Not only did it remove the tattoo, it removed his upper arm as well. A true vanishing cream. Equally miraculously, his upper arm faded back into full visibility within four hours. While all this was happening to his body, the inventor was watching television: a police rescue squad was called to an LA fast-food restaurant to airlift a rock star to safety. The inventor next showered with the potion, becoming totally invisible. He added the potion to the clothes washer, rendering his jeans and T shirt invisible. Then he walked invisibly past security at the superstar's Bel Air estate, ambled through his mansion and met him in his study. During their initial meeting, the inventor faded back in from invisibility. Convinced by the stunning demonstration, the superstar tried it for himself. Thirty minutes later, the invisible superstar and the visible inventor were back at McDonalds's for the superstar's Big Mac. And so the tale unfolded, as the writer pitched his screen story to the mesmerized Missy...

"I love it! The concept, the story, the ending. All of it. How'd you like to meet Michael Jackson?"

The meeting was set for the following Wednesday at 9 p.m. at Studio One on Ventura Boulevard in Burbank, where the singer was mixing his *History* album. Missy greeted him in the reception area.

"You know, a busload of volunteers wanted to accompany me here tonight. I could have sold a ton of tickets."

She laughed. Teller looked over at a beefy security person. Security nodded impassively. A second blue-jacketed person opened a nearby door and in they went.

They entered what appeared to be a large well-kept living room: sofa, armchairs, a coffee table with bowls of nuts and vegetarian items, several paintings on the walls of idyllic Renaissance scenes, large floor-based stereo monitors, and now walking over to greet them: the most famous entertainer on the planet. Michael Jackson was taller than the writer expected, at six feet plus the bowler hat. Dressed entirely in black: silk shirt, designer trousers, dress shoes. It was the early nineties, and the star's features and complexion were unaltered by cosmetic surgery, with the exception of the nose, which was somewhat trimmer than in his childhood photographs. The eyes were large, unwavering, friendly, with the modestly confident look of one who enjoyed immediate admiration in every daily encounter.

An unmistakably childlike warmth radiated across to the visitor.

"The storyteller—live and in person..." said the famous high-pitched voice.

The hand, when shaken, was like a thin bag of chicken bones.

"I don't mean to be ordinary, but I've been a huge fan for years."

Michael Jackson's smile broadened. "That never gets ordinary. Thank you," said the star.

Teller had seen his share of stars and had met several. But never anything like this. He was surprised at the intensity of his own reaction. He felt an unmistakable adrenaline rush—stronger than the one he experienced when skydiving. The performer he had seen so many times on video and on television was—in this intimate setting—every bit as electrifying. They sat down.

"Something to drink?" asked the singer.

"I'm fine."

"Michael heard the short version of *Invisible* from me, but he would very much like to hear the unabridged version directly from the writer himself," said Missy.

The singer smiled. "Missy is so totally Ivy League. Don't you just love her?"

The writer got to work.

"OK, we're in a movie theatre with a thousand others—room lights down, screen lights up on a beautiful low aerial shot somewhere in LA. Palm trees and traffic flickering by below us—seen from the point of view of a SkyCam TV reporter—as we come upon a huge commotion in the parking lot of a fast-food restaurant. A celebration? A disaster? We move in closer..."

Twenty minutes later, Teller had taken them through the story highlights of *Invisible*. The madcap inventor sharing his four-hour vanishing cream with the rock star, the invisible adventures that opened up for the superstar, the bad guys chasing them to steal the formula to commit invisible crimes, recovering the formula, the superstar's crisis when he suddenly goes permanently invisible, to the pair racing for an antidote, the superstar learning an invaluable life lesson—and on to the surprise ending.

Then: silence.

Michael Jackson let the moment hang suspended. "You're such a good storyteller. I have that fantasy all the time," he said.

The writer did his best to conceal a huge feeling of relief. His deal of a lifetime was now on track.

"But tell me now—*Invisible* is not a musical, right?" said the singer.

"I don't write musicals—wouldn't know how," said Teller.

"Thank you, Lord, for bringing this screenplay to me!" said the singer. "Hey, ever notice the only singers who made it big in the movies never sang? Sinatra—academy award for *From Here to Eternity*? Dean Martin in those fine old westerns like *Rio Bravo*? Jimmy Cagney and his great gangster films? Never sang. And the biggest rock star of them all—who did sing on screen—did twenty musicals nobody remembers. I'm after the movie career Elvis never had. "

"Michael is very committed to developing the right screenplay," said Missy. "Everything begins there."

"Believe it," said the singer. "The album I'm mixing here: it's called *History*. That's no accident. I've been doing the music thing 25 years now. I'm hitting my late thirties. All that shuckin' and jivin' up on stage with those young dancers gonna wear you out! The right screen role in the right story is the next chapter for me. With your help, man."

"There's nothing I'd rather be doing," said the writer. "Let the pitching begin! First stop: Columbia Pictures."

Back home, dinner conversation was electric.

"Wow—You really met Michael Jackson, Dad? Is he nice?" said the boy.

"Yes, very friendly."

"And he's going to be in your movie?"

"We'll see. It takes a little while to write these things and get them going—but Michael's definitely on board." said Teller.

"Jackie Manning's desk is still empty. Please tell Michael: he can come to school with me while you're writing."

When the writer relocated to Hollywood two years earlier, he was struck by the unique Hollywood system of selling stories to the studios: pitching. A writer with a movie story would link up with a producer, director or movie star. His agent would then arrange for him to personally pitch his story to a studio executive. The ideal creative combination was writer/ irresistible story idea/ a significant star ready to commit to it. If the pitch was successful, the studio would buy the story on the spot and commission the writer to do the screenplay on a fixed schedule. With Michael Jackson committed to the project, they were in a very strong position. Michael had a "first look" deal with Columbia who provided him with office space and paid for his staff, including Missy. Accompanied by her, the writer pitched to an audience of three: Columbia Pictures' vice president of production, a high-level associate and an assistant who took rapid notes. Studio pitches were completely verbal: no written summaries were given. At stake was an immediate script development deal in the $250,000 range, with the prospect of a movie commitment worth from $30 to $50 million.

They were received with elaborate courtesy in a lavish beige office. The meeting lasted an unhurried fifty minutes. It took forty-eight hours to get a response from the studio, and it was: "No, thanks."

"I don't believe it!" said the writer to Missy on the phone. "Columbia has a deal with you guys to make a movie! Did they give a reason?"

"The story doesn't fit his image."

"Excuse me," said Teller. "His image? Who are they to sit in judgment on that? Isn't image something for Michael and you and the film's director and maybe the writer to work on?"

"Apparently not," she said.

"No story notes? No request for a follow-up meeting?"

"No," she said.

"Who do these people think they are?!" said the incredulous writer.

"They think they're in charge," said Missy.

Pitch number two was at Disney; Agent Orange set this one up.

The writer and the D girl met at Disney's finely manicured Burbank campus with its period stucco and new sandstone buildings at the intersection of Mickey Way and Goofy Drive. Today's pitch was to two vice presidents. The writer noted the matching Rolexes.

Agent Orange noted their prompt response twenty-four hours later.

"Pass. Disney says they have a full slate right now."

"Oh, really?" said Teller. "Then why'd they take the pitch?"

"I think what's really going on here is they have a couple of projects of their own they want to pitch Michael, and they just wanted to meet his D girl. We sorta got used," said Agent Orange.

"I don't know what to say," said Teller.

"Don't worry about it!" said Agent Orange. "Every door in Hollywood's open to us. Just keep visualizing opening night! I'm brushing up my moonwalking moves already!"

Pitch number three was at Paramount Pictures on Melrose Avenue in the heart of old Hollywood. The buildings had the look of large 1930s public high schools. They arrived at the office of Paramount's senior VP of production: Mr. Friendly. The perfect surname.

"If you don't mind my asking, is that a stage name?" asked the writer.

The exec chuckled indulgently from the other side of an immaculate mahogany desk. "If so, my father never told me."

Two days later, the benign principal of Hollywood High passed on *Invisible*. Agent Orange delivered the news. "Don't worry about it! That guy's on his way out: it's all over Hollywood. Hey—Michael's girl just called. Can you can come by the recording studio for a meet at 9 tonight?"

The King of Pop saw the concern on his writer's face. "You mustn't worry. The money always shows up—sooner or later," said the high-pitched voice.

"It's been a little surprising, that's all," said Teller.

Missy interjected. "We asked you over because a certain aspect of the story has been on Michael's mind."

Michael Jackson leaned forward. "OK—the lead character, this star who longs for a few normal hours in public—meets this madcap inventor—who comes up with a temporary vanishing cream—star gets to live out his invisible fantasy for a few hours at a time…"

"Exactly," said the writer.

The singer rose and paced. "But here's the thing. How does the audience know I'm in the scene when I'm invisible? Objects I touch move around on their own, right? Or I wear regular clothes and a mask like the Phantom of the Opera—right?"

The writer nodded.

"But wouldn't the studio want the audience to see me in those scenes? Like—they're paying for me to be up on screen?"

"The audience will suspend its disbelief. It's a movie," said the writer.

Yet clearly they were having a problem in selling the movie, which the singer had been grappling with.

"I've got another approach to the whole invisible thing," Michael said. "Ever watch those old black and white movies from the thirties and forties that have been colorized? Slick technology. So—how about if we shoot my invisible scenes in black and white, then in post-production, color everything back in—except invisible me? I stay black and white; everything else in the scene is color."

The idea sank in. "It's perfect; totally visual!" said the writer.

"It might help us get this thing going," said the singer.

"Thank you," said Missy.

On his way out, the writer produced an 8 by 10 glossy of his son pulling a Radio Flyer wagon and wearing a cap with "Michael" on the brim.

"You've got more than one fan in our family," said Teller.

"That's sweet," said Michael.

The star reached down for the ever-present Sharpie indelible pen on the coffee table.

Pitch number four was set for Universal Studios in Burbank with a new vice president of development looking to make her mark. As with each previous executive, she proclaimed herself a huge fan of the singer. The writer elaborated the storyline, including the black and white colorization device.

"That's very creative. The director will have a field day," said the executive.

She would take *Invisible* directly to the president of the studio.

The response came forty-eight hours later.

"But she said she loved it!" said the writer.

"She does," said Missy on the phone. "Here's the problem: she wouldn't right come out and say it directly, but the head of the studio's an old guy—been around a very long time…"

"So?" said the writer.

"So, he's worried Michael wouldn't be accepted by certain demographics—certain parts of the country—as a movie star, and especially in a romantic scene. He's worried about the kiss."

"Hold on," said Teller. "This is the biggest pop star in the world! He transcends that tired old racist crap!"

"Yes, he does. But not for everybody. And this particular gentleman is just a couple of decades behind that curve."

—∞—

Fall turned to winter beneath an ever-blue California sky; Agent Orange's enthusiasm for *Invisible* was steadfast.

"Stay focused! Stay positive! He's a superstar! This thing's gonna happen!"

"How about putting me up for a writing assignment—you know, grocery money?" said the writer.

"Hang in there! Get *Invisible* set up and you'll be buying the whole supermarket," said the agent. "Remember now: if he invites you to any holiday parties, I get to tag along, OK?"

Three more pitches; three more rejections. They had run out of studios to pitch. Agent Orange was on the phone.

"Meet me at the lounge at the Beverly Wilshire at 6, OK?"

"I could use a drink," said Teller.

The Polynesian waitress delivered a dazzling smile and a pair of Mai Tais.

The agent raised his glass. "Here's to the fork in the road," he said.

They sipped.

"Which one?" said Teller.

"Ours," said Agent Orange. "We're heading in separate directions. Good luck."

"What?" said the former client.

Agent Orange laid it out. "This whole thing's made me look bad. I'm the agent who can't sell the Michael Jackson project."

"So? What percentage of pitches sells overall? Ten—fifteen?" said the writer.

"Not the point. This one should have sold. We were all surprised," said Agent Orange.

"And I get to be the fall guy?" said the writer.

The agent silently sipped his Mai Tai.

"Why didn't you package my story with a name producer, or an A-list director, or a co-star for the inventor role? I asked you to. Studios like packages. They get projects going," said Teller.

"Didn't seem necessary for something this high-profile," said the agent.

"Still feel that way?" said the writer.

Agent Orange shifted in his rattan chair. "Hindsight's a bitch," he said.

An hour later, Missy called.

"How you doing?" she asked.

"I feel like I didn't come through for Michael. After he supported my story—met with me—attached his name to it," said the writer.

Missy listened. "If it makes you feel any better, he has a ton of stuff going on all the time. And he's not a guy to sit around blaming or regretting."

"I hope so," said the writer.

"He asked me to tell you something," she said. "He loves this story. When the money eventually catches up with you, and a studio is ready —he'll still be there."

"Oh, man…" said Teller.

"Just don't turn it into a musical, OK?"

"Deal!" he said.

They laughed.

Darkness descended on the cozy bungalow in Venice Beach, where the autographed superstar photo hung on the wall of a child's bedroom.

"So you and Michael won't be making the movie together?" said the boy.

"Not this year, anyway," said the dad. It was bedtime.

"Are you sad?" said the boy.

"It's only fame and money."

"But doesn't everybody want that?" asked the son.

"Well, wanting and getting aren't the same things. The important thing is never giving up."

The boy looked up from his pillow. "Now you can come to school with me and take Jackie Manning's desk."

Dad smiled. "Young man, *you* never give up."

"Tomorrow, Dad! We'll play basketball with Tony Baloney."

"I'll visit you guys at recess: how's that?" said the writer.

"All right!"

They high-fived.

"Story time. Lights out in fifteen," said the writer.

"We're starting a new one tonight, Dad. We finished *Treasure Island* last night. What's next?"

"One about a young inventor who comes up with a marvelous new invention," said Teller.

The boy's eyes glowed.

"Do people get excited when they first see it? Like with Tom Edison and the electric light?"

"Excited? They can't believe their eyes! It's magical," said Teller.

"Tell me the title."

"*Invisible.*"

"Cool," said the boy. "Sometimes when I'm going off to sleep I feel invisible, but in the morning when I wake up—there I am all over again."

The writer smiled. "Hey! Who's telling this story anyway?"

The boy grinned and burrowed deeper into his comforter; the story began.

It was the best of times.

The End

… of an unforgettable encounter.

FROM GERMANY WITH LOVE
Still Man's Best Friend

Each Monday through Friday at 8:15 a.m., she descended into the 23rd Street subway station in New York's Flatiron District, boarded the Number 6 South, and emerged seven minutes later at her vintage skyscraper in the heart of the Financial District. **But not this morning.** Today she headed north, clattering under the restaurants, the galleries, the theatres, the feet of the quarter million tourists, the bike and horse paths of the great park, the field of dreams of the great stadium, on to the 140th Street station and up its time-worn stairway to the Bronx. Behind her, step by tedious step, she pulled a 75-pound wheeled suitcase.

"Can I lend a hand?" A well-groomed man in his late thirties smiled reassuringly: The World's Greatest City showing its decent side.

"Thank you. That would be a great help."

He took the heavy brown case, quickening his pace. "Heading off on vacation?" he asked over his shoulder.

The attractive, care-laden woman in her early forties responded, "I wish…"

The Good Samaritan emerged into the sunshine at the top of the stairwell, well ahead of her despite the heavy suitcase. She noted his fitness and her own lack of it. The idea of walking to work for exercise: one of the many good intentions parked in the waiting room of her life. She called after him. "Thank you very much. So nice of you—excuse me—wait for me—Hey—Stop! Come back!"

Vanished, a shadow in the noonday crowd.

"Thief! Thief!"

A good deed turned bad in a New York minute.

—m—

Fifteen minutes later, the bad Samaritan stepped down from a cross-town bus in front of a seedy rent-controlled walk-up. "Lady, you luggin' some heavy gear around this town," he muttered to himself. He climbed to the fourth level and stopped at a smudged apartment door triple-locked against those like himself. Rolling his prize inside, he collapsed into a La-Z-Boy lounger.

"Ooo wee! How cool is me!" Digging into the secret recesses of the chair, he extracted a fat spliff that would do Snoop Dogg proud. An agrecable haze soon filled his lungs and shabby hideaway.

> *"Fee-fie-fo-fum*
> *I smell the scent*
> *Of treasure to come!"*

The anticipation of unearned income elicited a cackle, followed by a second massive inhale/exhale.

> *"Shoulda been a poet*
> *Cause my feet both show it*
> *They both be Longfellows*
> *And smell like the Dickens!"*

Rising from his reverie, he pulled a pair of pliers from a kitchen drawer, snapped the suitcase lock and laid his treasure chest on its side. With a performer's flourish, he unzipped the top of the case and flung it open. The contents sprang forth into the room three seconds slower than the terrified man fleeing it. The snarling German shepherd, stiff from his extreme confinement, gave his liberator the head start necessary to bolt into the bathroom, slam the door shut, and wedge his shoulder against it.

"Jesus Christ! Holy Shit! Mary, Mother of God! Help me!"

The frothing beast on the other side slammed repeatedly against the bathroom door. The thief dug into his pocket, extracted an iPhone and dialed.

"Come on—answer the damn phone, Phil—come on!!"

Brothers are made for such emergencies, though they might prefer otherwise.

Phil answered. "You're calling to come by and pay me back, right? Right?"

To convince anyone you are held captive in your own bathroom by a snarling German shepherd inches from your throat is a challenge. The situation has the ring of April Fools, an LSD hallucination, an extreme bipolar episode—too strange.

"You gotta get over here right away, Phil! For God's sake! You're a dog walker! They like you! Animals never liked me! You know that!"

"You know why they don't like you, right? They smell insincerity. Selfishness. They know you'll forget to feed them. And pull their tails. They've got your number, Brother."

The thief was saucer-eyed with fear. "Whatever you say, Bro! Just listen to this!" He held the iPhone against the bathroom door. The rage from the other side had reached the intensity of a braying Middle Eastern mob at their toppled ruler's hideaway.

—⁂—

Thirty minutes later, the dog walker was in the shabby apartment hand-feeding the docile German. The rescuer was senior to his thieving sibling, with the calm demeanor of those who work with animals.

"Careful, Phil! Watch your fingers!"

"He's an old boy. No worries. "

"Ha! Old Killer, you mean! From a stiff to a killer!"

"He was probably in a coma. Happens to animals, too. Owner was probably taking him to the pet cemetery in the upper Bronx when Boy Scout comes along."

The thief was downcast. "Why me? Hey? Why me?"

"You really want to know?" said his rescuer. "Because you're a thieving a-hole. That's why. "

The German began licking the dog walker's face.

"Look at him! Slobbering over you straight after trying to kill me! I'm taking his old ass to the pound."

"Oh, really? And what if the owner's there looking for him and recognizes you?"

This gave the thief pause.

"Got a point there. You take him!"

"And what if the owner's given him up for dead and never shows up? Which is more likely. What happens to him then?"

The bad brother smiled. "There are eight million stories in the Naked City."

"He's your responsibility," said Phil.

"Bro, you're the doggie expert, not me. Tell you what: here, take my iPhone. It's brand new. It costs $500. Use it to call the ladies while you're walking Old Fang. Juice up your love life, man! You've been living alone for too long. Find yourself a nice two-legged friend!"

"Tell you what: you worry about your life—I'll worry about mine."

A sibling rivalry without end.

"OK, I'll keep his shaggy ass. I'll just have to take him for a little stroll down the street, won't I? Let's hope Old Fang doesn't get dazed and confused and wander into traffic..."

Phil got up and paced his brother's seedy apartment. "You know what I really need?" he said.

"You need to track down that owner. Reunite Fang with his people. Pick up some good karma. And I'll still throw in the iPhone!"

Phil looked down at his deeply flawed sibling. "That's not what I need," he said.

"Tell me what you need, Bro. Maybe I can score it for you. I got connections."

The answer came from a place of insufferably long experience. "What I need—is to be reborn as an only child. Never again to be dragged into the depressing, ever-darkening pit you call your life. This is what I need."

The words were received in the typical manner.

"That is—just your opinion, Bro."

—៳—

The dog walker left with the dog and a plan. The lady with the fateful suitcase had emerged at the 140th Street station from the 6 North. He reasoned her journey began on the 6 South, possibly as far down as Battery Park. Between there and 140th Street were six doggie parks maintained by the city. He would bring the German to each one until he was recognized and ultimately reunited with his owner.

The next morning, both brothers missed an intriguing local TV news story featuring an interview at the 140th Street subway entrance.

"Please," the woman begged, "I just want to send Fritz off to his final rest in peace. Whoever took the suitcase—or whoever finds him inside—please, just bring him to the Bronx Pet Cemetery. No questions asked, and a $300 reward gladly paid."

The reporter spoke squarely into the camera. "You heard it first here on ABC 7. Step up, Big City! Show that big heart of yours. Help us bring Fritz home to the Bronx Pet Cemetery. His owner—and a $300 reward—are waiting. Bring Fritz home!" The reporter checked his earpiece. "Now, I understand we're going to City Hall: the mayor has a statement..."

New York's top dog faced a dozen reporters in a hastily-called press conference. "I'm a dog lover myself—two yellow Labs. There are over 800,000 canines in Greater New York. A testament to our humane and caring side. Which is why the Greatest City is now offering a $2,000 no-questions-asked reward so that Fritz—God rest his soul—may be returned to his owner and given a proper send-off."

The next day, Phil's plan was in motion. New Yorkers and their pets hit the doggy parks en masse promptly after 5 p.m. Phil would visit two parks an evening for the rest of the week, bringing the rejuvenated German to six parks within three days. They began with Battery Park. No luck. Then on to Washington Square Park, divided into separate facilities for small and large animals. They entered the large animal section, where they were immediately greeted by a collie, a St. Bernard, and a rescue greyhound in the company of an anorexic former model.

"He's so sweet." She patted the old dog.

"Do you recognize him by any chance?"

"Should I? Is he famous?" she asked playfully.

"No, but you probably are..." he said with a smile.

"Not anymore—fame comes and goes, does it not? Like yesterday's newspapers and magazines."

"Better to be loved than famous," said Phil.

"That's where the dogs come in," said the model. "I've always found it a lot easier to find a good dog than a good man in this city."

The dogs interrupted the conversation with a mad race around the perimeter of the park. Not surprisingly, the greyhound won. Phil smiled. "Old New York has a way of surprising people if they give it a chance."

The next evening found Phil at the busiest doggie park: Union Square at 14th Street, where Edison hung the world's first electric streetlights. The German immediately hit it off with a playful Maltese.

"Isn't that something? He thinks your dog is his old pal Fritz," said the owner of the Maltese, an older gentleman who clearly spent time at Brooks Brothers.

"Why would he think that, I wonder?" said Phil.

"Try explaining to a dog that his old pal from Germany has simply disappeared after all these years. Vanished. He won't hear of it."

"When did he disappear?" asked Phil.

"About a week ago," said the gentleman from Brooks.

"If you don't mind my asking—where did his vanished friend reside?" said Phil.

Twenty minutes later, Phil and the German were strolling the iron-fenced perimeter of Gramercy Park, the last keyed private park in Manhattan. A sidewalk flagstone indicated its founding in 1841: a world apart from Manhattan then and now. A resident walking her Rhodesian Ridgeback paused as the dogs greeted each other like old friends.

"He looks just like his old pal Fritz," she said.

"So I've been hearing," said Phil. "And where did Fritz live, I wonder?" he asked as casually as possible. She pointed towards a venerable sandstone structure with brown granite columns. Fritz strained at his leash—clearly elated to be home again. "Easy, Boy—easy." Phil stood before the building, reading the plaques honoring famous former residents including Peck and Cagney.

"Well, well—don't you look familiar!"

The German peered up the front entry stairs into the friendly face of an impeccably dressed doorman. He came down the steps to pat the dog, by now in spasms of delight.

"They say we all have a double walking the Earth somewhere," said the doorman.

"The Germans call it our doppelgänger," said Phil.

"Would you mind if I buzzed someone upstairs for a quick meet and greet?" said the doorman.

Five minutes later, the lady with the fateful suitcase appeared. She was charmed and delighted but unaware of the full significance of the moment.

"Why, he's just like my dear departed old Fritz! It's almost too much. What's his name?"

"May we speak in private for a moment?" said Phil.

She led the way to a spacious downstairs reception room; the doorman drew the tall doors shut. There Phil informed her of the true situation, omitting his thieving brother and claiming he had come upon the suitcase abandoned on the sidewalk. The joyous reunion prompted an invitation to the lady's residence on the eighth floor overlooking venerable Gramercy Park.

Phil found himself in the largest apartment he had ever entered. There was actually room for an indoor city stroll. Pictures of a major movie star from the fifties and sixties were clearly in evidence, as was the resemblance to his daughter who had inherited the apartment.

"It's like Fritz has just returned from the other side. Unbelievable! People go into comas of course, but you don't expect it with animals," she said.

"He was very happy to wake up. After a brief adjustment period."

"What sort of adjustment?" she asked with concern.

"Oh, a little misunderstanding with—the mailman, that's all. It blew over."

"Well, all I can say is your mailman must not like dogs, and Fritz sensed that. He's an excellent judge of people," she said.

"So I've noticed," said Phil.

"That's why he was happy to stay with you," she said, smiling warmly.

"He caught me on a good day," said Phil modestly.

He explained his plan to reunite Fritz with his owner by systematically bringing him to the doggy parks.

"So very generous—so thoughtful of you," she said warmly.

"I knew under the circumstances you wouldn't be searching for him at the animal shelters," said Phil.

"My poor Fritzy! I must tell the building staff here if anyone finds me unresponsive in bed one day not to jump to dark conclusions," she said.

They laughed.

Fritz had parked himself squarely in front of a large flat screen TV; he barked three times.

"Time for his show!"

She activated the Blu-ray remote, bringing to life a vintage Technicolor television show: *The Adventures of Rin Tin Tin*. "He's a huge fan," she said. "We've seen all 114 episodes. It's actually quite clever."

"My little guy prefers chasing skateboards and squirrels," said Phil.

"Charming. What breed?"

"Jack Russell."

"Oh, they're highly intelligent," she said.

"As are the Germans," he said.

"So we'd best keep them apart; they could gang up on us," she said.

They smiled. Pause. But not awkward.

"There's this bottle of rather good bubbly I've been saving for some occasion or other," she said.

Phil smiled. "My father sent me out into this world with two pieces of advice: pay your taxes on time and never say 'No' to champagne."

"Clearly a wise man," she said.

Their eyes met and held. A champagne cork popped. Bubbly bubbled. Fritz barked a blessing. **Nightfall began its starry descent in the city that never sleeps.**

Das Ende

… of living out of a suitcase.

THE KING OF SMILES
A Brief History of Dentistry

Konigsberg was destined for dentistry, but that never meant he had to embrace it. He came from a seriously long line of drillers and fillers—father, uncle, grand-uncle, a smattering of cousins, and a foster child on his mother's side. All having done very nicely by dentistry, thank you very much. The family career path for Konigsberg was paved, preordained, prepaid, and completely unappealing. His true love was the movies, and Hollywood's portrayal of dentistry hit him hard from an early age.

The celluloid shit-kicking began with Chaplin's *Laffing Gas* (1914), in which a cruel dentist sedated his patient with a club. W.C. Fields continued Hollywood's sadistic tradition with *The Dentist* (1932), wherein the bulky comedian straddled a female patient strapped to the chair, working her over with a nasty pair of pliers sans anesthetic. The seventies brought forth *The Boys from Brazil*, featuring the acclaimed Laurence Olivier as a dentist turned Nazi torturer. Ten years later, the goofy Steve Martin groped a beautiful dental patient in *Little Shop of Horrors* (1986), then found himself being fed to a carnivorous plant. All of which struck young Konigsberg as embarrassing at best, revolting at worst. He told his father as much.

"You don't become a dentist for entertainment value, Alan. You want entertainment, marry a nice girl who cooks and plays piano," said Dr. K Sr.

"At the same time?" said Konigsberg the younger.

"Such a kidder! Save it for some salaried schmo who needs a laugh. Me, I'm already laughing—all the way to the bank."

"I'm happy for you, Dad. It's just not for me."

Famous last words. He graduated from the UCLA School of Dentistry in 1987 and entered the family business. His graduation present: a Triumph TR6 convertible, delivery to be taken in England— followed by a one-month solo tour of Europe, top down, radio up. He packed three changes of clothes and thirty pairs of underwear and socks and hopped an overnight flight from JFK to Heathrow. It was glorious. He grew a trim brown moustache and goatee that would stay with him. He would replay the highlights of the Grand Tour in the lively theatre of his memory for decades to come: buskers in the streets and subways of London, dawn breaking over the Tuileries sculpture garden in Paris, the cheapest restaurant in Europe on a Lisbon side street, the operating theatre in the main bullring in Madrid, the topless beaches of Cannes where aspiring actresses covered their nipples with Perrier caps, the restaurateur's daughter from Seattle who shared his bed from Istanbul to Belgrade, the blues club overlooking the Charles Bridge in Prague where Ray Charles ruled from a vintage Wurlitzer, the cornball polka bands of Bavaria, the graciousness of the Dutch, the hydrofoil hovering back to England, and finally the return trip to America where destiny awaited.

His father couldn't help noticing the old lack of enthusiasm.

"All right, what would you rather do? Let's get it out in the open," he said.

"Be an actor. I think I might be good at it," Konigsberg Jr. said.

The bald, gray older man looked at him wearily. "That again? Still? Know what I've always wanted to do? Become an astronaut. But none of that circle the Earth or visit the moon stuff—I always wanted to visit Saturn! Check out those pretty rings up close. Wouldn't that be something? Meanwhile, waiting for that big call from NASA, there was a living to earn."

Young Konigsberg didn't crack a shadow of a smile. The older man's expression softened. "Look, Son, maybe you could combine the two—dentistry and the movies. Set up your practice in LA—specialize in the cosmetic side—all those actors and actresses with their million-dollar smiles—dentist to the stars. How about that?"

Konigsberg set up shop on trendy Montana Avenue in Santa Monica. He crowned himself the King of Smiles, with local newspaper and bus stop ads featuring him in full dentist's regalia topped by a jewel-encrusted crown. A starring role all his own. The ads worked; actors, directors, models and more than a few porn stars showed up daily in his waiting room. Approved by the health plans of the Screen Actors Guild, the Directors Guild, the Writers Guild, and the Producers Association—he was in business. Soon there were warmly autographed photos of grinning clients on the wall to prove it.

The King of Smiles promoted his new image relentlessly, hiring a top LA car painter to transform the TR6 convertible into a gleaming white number 4 bicuspid, his web address across each door: www. kingofsmiles.com. His office gave out tooth-shaped business cards. Konigsberg displayed a natural promotional flair. Women approached him in supermarkets, soliciting his opinion on their smiles. Children ogled him on the sidewalk: "Mommy, Mommy—it's the King of Smiles! Look!"

But combining dentistry and show business became a forced thing: an arranged marriage without love. He tried to make it work.

"How did you get started in the business?" he would ask the actress or director in the chair.

"Aaaaargh, nngrrllt, rbsttt," came the reply through the dental apparatus.

He stopped asking. It rankled that the King of Smiles' celebrity was entirely local, confined to the bus stop ads and the *Santa Monica Daily Press*. He longed for a larger audience.

Meanwhile, LA's never-ending quest for the perfect smile made him rich, then richer, then finally the richest in his family. Still, there was something missing at the core of it all. His dreams of artistic fulfillment and public recognition were steadily slipping away with the passage of time: until that spring evening he stepped inside his local Blockbuster Video and received a fateful movie recommendation.

"Trust me, Dr. K—you'll love it! *Amadeus* even has a king in it like you. And it won eight Academy Awards!"

"OK, I'll take it."

"Can I ask you a question, Dr. K?" She was young and pretty.

"What about my smile? Like, what would it take to realign these four upper front ones?" She bared all. What it took was a month of concentrated dental work and heavy dating. Which was totally fine— but the movie recommendation was not so fine. He hated *Amadeus* with a surprising passion, yet couldn't take his eyes off it. He replayed the film compulsively.

"Goddamn piece of shit!" Konigsberg yelled at his Sony Trinitron.

The offender wasn't the young Mozart with his financial and family crises. Not at all. The offender was Mozart's untalented, unrecognized nemesis Salieri deriding Mozart from an insane asylum. As a composer, he fell far short of Mozart and was well aware of it. His inescapable mediocrity and lack of public recognition ate away at the composer. From the asylum, he crowned himself Patron Saint of the Mediocre, Avatar of the Average, spokesman for the mildly talented, keenly aware he would never compose in the "god-like manner" of Mozart. Salieri's dilemma was too close to home for Konigsberg.

"Asshole! Self-hater! Loser!" he screamed at the Trinitron with the Dolby surround sound and advanced comb filter. By the fourth viewing, the King of Smiles came undone. In a proper rage, he arose from the sofa, went to his winter storage closet, pulled out his right ski boot, clumped back to the TV room, and drove that boot straight through *Amadeus* and the big screen. The TV smashed, sparked, discombobulated. "Yes! Yes!" shouted Konigsberg, executing a club-footed victory dance around the living room.

Next morning found the King of Smiles uncommonly chipper. Receptionist Bonny noticed immediately.

"Why, Doctor K, you're like the cat who swallowed the canary," she said.

He smiled serenely. But by Thursday, the blues were upon him again like an old debt. The soul-sapping nature of his dental career dogged him. What path to public recognition and inner peace was left? Larger acts of destruction? Firebomb the studio that concocted the foul *Amadeus*? The vengeful fantasies alarmed him. He was awakening screaming in the middle of the night, his top-of-the-line Beautyrest soaked in sweat. The King of Smiles was approaching a total nervous breakdown.

Then the Baxters showed up. Baxter Sr. was a tall thirty-something screenwriter, with an eleven-year-old son at his side. Dr. K got right down to it.

"A screenwriter? Would I know any of your movies?"

"Not yet. I'm in Development Hell," the writer said.

"What's that?" said the dentist.

"Development Hell is where the studios or producers buy your stories—but no green light. No movie deal. Never-never land."

"You get paid anyway?" asked Dr. K.

"Six figures. How else could I afford the King of Smiles? The only thing worse than Development Hell is not being in Development Hell. No deal at all." A gold-paved dead end.

Dr. K returned to the business at hand. "And how can we help young Mr. Baxter today?"

Blond slack-jawed Baxter Jr. stared up at the dentist, revealing a rogue canine protruding well above the normal gum line. An extra tooth with no room to grow. A blemish on the boy's California-perfect looks.

"An atypical condition. Has to come out," said the King of Smiles.

"Can I take it home?" said the boy.

"Of course, it's your tooth! Now Mr. Baxter, why don't we have a quick look at you?"

Five minutes later, Dr. K completed his examination: six cavities, an upper left front root canal, a chipped lower right bicuspid, advanced gum disease.

"Your teeth are in terrible shape, Baxter."

"People call me Teller."

"Why do they call you that?"

"I guess because I tell stories for a living."

"Right now, I'm more interested in what you've been eating."

"Shit and plenty of it. I'm a writer in Development Hell, remember?"

That night at 3:10 a.m., the King of Smiles awoke with a Big Idea involving the Baxters. Six hours later, receptionist Bonny was summoning the writer in for a free cleaning, courtesy of the King.

"Now, this is what I call service!" opined the supine scribe from the hygienist's chair.

"Let's just say I have a soft spot for Hollywood," said Dr. K. "Baxter, how would you like to help your son, help yourself, and make medical history in the process?"

"Sounds like a win-win-win," said the writer.

"Well said! Back in the sixties, Dr. Christiaan Barnard did the first heart transplant. Became world famous! Since then, we've seen kidney transplants, liver transplants, heart-lung transplants and now full facial transplants," said the dentist.

"Don't forget hair transplants. Good old Doc Bosley. Famous all over Hollywood," said Baxter.

"But what we have *not* yet seen is a tooth transplant," said Konigsberg.

"Drum roll, please!" said the writer.

"Listen, Baxter: that bad upper left canine of yours is in the exact same position as your son's rogue canine that must come out. Here's the idea: the two of you go simultaneously into separate treatment rooms. We remove your bad tooth and clean and prep the hole left in the gum. Then I extract your son's good tooth nerve and all, and immediately implant it in you. The world's first live tooth transplant! Since you're father and son the chances of rejection are low. You come by for a weekly X-ray to make sure it's being accepted. You get a beautiful healthy new tooth, your son gets back his great smile, we all make dental history.

Oh, and I get famous: an article in the *Journal of the American Dental Association* and coverage all over the Internet."

Konigsberg was practically levitating with excitement.

"What's the tab?" asked Baxter.

"Nothing. Nada. Zilch," said the King of Smiles.

"I'm in," said the scribe.

—∞—

Seconds after the writer and his son left, Konigsberg was on the phone to his father.

"I am so proud of you, Alan," said the dad. "You are doing nothing less than making dental history. All I ever did was make an obscene amount of money. You're shooting for much more. You'll be famous, just like those Hollywood people you're working on every day. This is fantastic!" said the old driller and filler.

—∞—

"So what do you think of that dentist gentleman?" Sr. asked Jr. as they strolled down Santa Monica's Third Street Promenade.

"Kinda average," said the boy.

"Average? Like he's not Brad Pitt?" said the dad. "Let me tell you, Son, Dr. K is definitely not your average dentist."

"Just say it, Dad. I know when you're leading up to something," said the boy.

So he told him about the tooth transplant.

"That Doc's out of his freaking mind! No! No way! That's creepy!"

"Since when is helping your old man creepy"? said Baxter.

"He's some kind of Dr. Frankenstein, moving people's body parts around and stuff," said the boy.

"You've been watching too many movies," said Baxter.

"Where'd I get that from?" said the boy.

"Listen, Mister, you're losing the tooth anyway. Nobody's stealing it from you."

"Really, Dad? How much you want to pay me for it?"

"My own son! I feed you, clothe you, educate you, buy you video games. Now I gotta pay for an unwanted tooth?"

"Dad, you always say: take care of your money and your money will take care of you. Right? That's all I'm doing—taking care of the money. That'll be a hundred dollars."

"Outrageous! The transplant might not work. My body might reject it. What then?"

"Your transplant—your rejection—not my problem," said the eleven-year-old.

"You are tough! We're sending you to the Middle East next week to sort that mess out," said the dad.

"One more thing," said the boy. "Like you never start writing until your fee's in the bank? The hundred's up front."

"With a business approach like that, Son, you got a big career waiting for you as an agent, maybe even a studio head. Those guys get to be hard-asses 365 days a year instead of just one."

They strolled the sunny sidewalk in silence.

"There's an ATM up ahead," said Dad with a hint of pride. They cemented their deal with cash.

Three days later, the Baxters found themselves in dual dental chairs, prepped and ready for history. First the dentist removed Sr.'s decayed upper front canine.

"Say goodbye to an old friend," said Dr. K.

"*Adios, amigo*," said the writer.

The dentist moved smartly over to Jr.'s treatment room. Five minutes later, he was back with a healthy live replacement.

"It's perfect!" said the dentist.

"What did you expect?" said the proud dad.

Ten minutes later, the transplant was complete. The dentist handed a magnifying mirror to his patient.

"My God—it's amazing! A perfect match," marveled the recipient.

"We just made dental history," said the King of Smiles through a huge smile of his own.

The young donor quietly entered the room.

"Thank you for the tooth, Son. How are you feeling?"

The boy stood there, subdued. "Can we go home now?" he said.

The next month was the best of times for the pioneering trio. Dr. K was a pleasure. His nightmares of revenge-taking on the makers of *Amadeus* were mercifully gone, replaced by visions of media fame and professional honors. If fame came from dentistry rather than show business—so be it. The boy? $100 to the good, and back to the more important business of being an eleven year-old. And Dad? Delighted with his perfect new tooth, which was bringing unanticipated side benefits.

The writer's canny agent was scoring studio pitch meetings on the strength of the transplant. First, he targeted execs who were parents to younger children. Second, he offered a unique sales pitch. Their first meeting was with MGM.

"Manny, you know I don't attend story pitches myself. But I had to introduce Baxter to you personally. He's a true pioneer."

The writer lifted his upper left lip and pointed to a tooth.

"It's a transplant. First one ever," said the agent.

"You mean an implant. Half of Hollywood's got those," said the VP.

"No, a transplant. That's his son's tooth, Manny. Excuse me—was his son's tooth until last week," said the agent.

The exec rounded his aircraft carrier-sized desk for a closer look. "Jesus! That's amazing! Congratulations!" said the VP.

"We're all about innovating," said the writer.

The agent seized the opening.

"Baxter's making medical history. But that's not what brings us to you today, Manny. He's got a story unique as that transplant; it'll knock your Hollywood socks off."

They didn't make the sale that day, but five pitches later they emerged from a meeting at Universal with $200,000 up front—first draft, rewrite, polish.

"They still love me in Development Hell…" said the writer.

The agent laughed. "Lunch on me! The Palm on Santa Monica Boulevard?"

—⁄⁄⁄—

Baxter slipped into the dentist's chair every Friday for his tissue compatibility X-ray.

"Don't they have pills to combat rejection?" he asked.

"Nasty side effects and they're not covered by your insurance," said Dr. K.

"What are my odds?" said Baxter.

"You've made it three weeks now with no problem, so I'm giving you 80:20 and improving daily."

"All right!" said Baxter, high-fiving the King of Smiles.

Good odds, but not quite good enough. Week four's X-ray bore the bad news: an ominous shadow in the bone surrounding the root. Tissue rejection. The transplant had to come out.

"Hang on. What if we just leave it in for a while longer and hope for the best? It's sort of a good luck charm for me," said the writer.

The King of Smiles frowned. "Seen a picture of Roger Ebert lately? Cancer of the jaw."

The writer returned home with a rueful gap-toothed grin.

"Aw, Dad—What happened?"

"Didn't really belong to me anyway, I guess. My body rejected it. Here..."

He handed over the tooth. The boy looked at it dejectedly. "Bummer. I told my friends at school; they thought it was super cool."

"I know," said Dad. "I got the same at work."

The boy looked surprised. "You did? You didn't mind running around the studios with a kid's tooth in your mouth?"

Baxter looked intently at his boy.

"Listen closely now. Number one: Your father never 'runs around' the studios. I walk—very cool—very in charge of myself. Number two: it was not just any kid's tooth. That was *my* son's tooth. A world of difference! I'm proud of what we did, and proud of the tooth! Understand?"

"Dad, I'm giving you back your hundred."

"No, Son. A deal's a deal, and men stand behind their deals. Just don't blow the cash, that's all. Keep it in the bank."

The sun went down over Santa Monica Boulevard, rising nine hours later from behind the Hollywood Hills. An eleven-year-old awakened, arose, then looked down at his pillow with reawakened interest. He flipped it over. In place of the rejected tooth secreted there the night before lay a glowing one-ounce American Buffalo gold coin. He picked it up in wonderment.

"Wakey wakey time in the old corral," said a familiar voice.

The boy turned to see his smiling gap-toothed father in the doorway.

"In my day, the tooth fairy brought nickels, dimes and quarters. You got the upgrade today," said Baxter.

The boy flashed a matching gap-toothed grin.

"Thanks, Dad. This is totally the best day," he said.

At that same moment, the King of Smiles was on the phone with his father, now 87 and in an East Coast retirement home.

"I'm sorry to hear that, Alan. It was a bold experiment, and I know it meant a lot to you," said the dental patriarch.

"I feel like such a failure, Pop," said the King of Smiles.

"What are you talking about?" said Konigsberg Sr. "You tried, didn't you? You aimed high! Just like Edison! That's what a man does! And I know you—you'll try again and again until it damn well works! **Then you'll be my son the famous dentist! Right? Damn right!** You make me proud! You got that, Son? You hearing your old man?"

There was a pause on the line from California. "Loud and clear. I love you, Dad," said Konigsberg.

The old man, a generation removed from emotional sharing, shifted uneasily in his wheelchair. "Enough with the love talk. Save it for some nice girl who cooks and plays piano. **It's still not too late for that, you know...**"

The End

... of a heady experiment.

ABOUT THE AUTHOR
RICK BUTLER

Author in Nova Scotia: Then   *Author in America: Now*

Author and entrepreneur Rick Butler, the son of an American-born mother and an Irish-born father, was raised in a Mountie household in small town Nova Scotia. He attended university in Ontario and England. He is the author of three books, two published by Doubleday, and numerous short stories. Two stories from this book were recently published in the literary journals, *The Antigonish Review* and *The Nashwaak Review*.

In previous lives, Rick was a radio and television announcer, a producer of TV drama and spoken word record albums, a Hollywood screenwriter, and, for seven years, a university professor. Many of the stories in this collection are based upon those real life experiences.

Rick is the owner of The Hotel California in Los Angeles and San Francisco (www.hotelca.com). He maintains residences in Los Angeles, Manhattan and Nova Scotia, where he lives with his wife and a trio of furry friends.

For live appearances or phone and email interviews:
rickbutlerassistant@gmail.com
Rick Butler may be contacted at:
hotelcaliforniadude@yahoo.com

CPSIA information can be obtained at www.ICGtesting.com
Printed in the USA
LVOW12s0504291013

358793LV00003B/95/P